AF279797

Zaraffel

Vol. 5 (2023)

Bibliografische Informationen der Deutschen Nationalbibliothek: Die Deutsche Nationalbibliothek verzeichnet diese Publikation in der Deutschen Nationalbibliografie; detaillierte bibliografische Daten sind im Internet über dnb.dnb.de abrufbar.

Herstellung und Verlag: BoD – Books on Demand, Norderstedt

AUSGABE 5, AUGUST 2023
Autoren: Mirona C., Stella Chachali, Georgios Dagkakis, Chen-Rui Eising, Erik Eising, Mark Farrier, Tim Redfern sowie blumenleere, SanforDKaraoke, Theo, Wayne Gibbous
Layoutentwicklung: Erik Eising
Gestaltung der Textrahmen: Mirona C., Stella Chachali, Chen-Rui Eising
Umschlagabbildung: Chen-Rui Eising & Erik Eising
Zaraffel Gruppe Berlin Kontakt:
Web: http://www.zaraffel-magazin.de
E-Mail: zaraffel@gmx.de

Titelfont ©Bloxy sowie ©Bloxy Stamped von *Mike™ Cox*; https://iprefermike.com/
Die Nutzung erfolgte mit freundlicher Genehmigung.

ISBN: 9783756898558

Dieses Magazin ist ein Ort zum Ausprobieren. In unseren Rubriken werden deutsch- und englischsprachige literarische Texte erstveröffentlicht. Bevor es erscheint, unterläuft jedes Heft drei kreative Schaffensphasen:

Eine neue Ausgabe beginnt mit der Konzeption der Rubrik **Kritzeleien**. Unsere Autorinnen und Autoren stellen dort jeweils einen Text vor, der sie thematisch gerade besonders beschäftigt. Gesammelt stellen sie einen Hauptteil des Magazins dar.

Im zweiten Teil beschäftigen sich *die Zaraffel* mit einem der Haupttexte. Die so enstehende Sammlung im **Echolot** kann als die experimentellste Rubrik des Magazins bezeichnet werden. Das liegt auch daran, dass die Texte Nachrufe auf Arbeiten aus älteren Ausgaben sein können. Sogar auf mehrere Texte gleichzeitig wurde bereits kreativ geantwortet. Woran man den Referenztext erkennt, wird zu Beginn der Rubrik kurz erläutert.

In jeder Ausgabe begrüßen die Zaraffel auch Gäste. Der **Taubenschlag** soll denjenigen, die ebenso wie wir dem literarischen Probieren verschrieben sind, eine Bühne bieten. In jeder Ausgabe wollen wir mehr und mehr talentierten oder bereits etablierten Kunstschaffenden die Möglichkeit geben, an Zaraffel teilzuhaben. Das ist eine Chance, gemeinsam zu wachsen.

Abgeschlossen wird jede Ausgabe im **Schlafittchen**. Dieser Teil bietet ausklingend jedem Mitglied im Wechsel die Möglichkeit, eine persönliche Arbeit im Detail vorzustellen oder einfach noch mehr Raum für Neues.

Unser Ziel ist ein Projekt, das seine eigene Entstehung und Weiterentwicklung kritisch begleitet. Was wir damit meinen, könnt ihr auch ausführlicher in unserer **Vision** lesen. Ihr findet sie nach dem Inhaltsverzeichnis und auf unserer Webseite.

~

Neugierig geworden? Dann scannt doch unseren QR-Code, besucht uns auf unserer Webseite oder kontaktiert uns via E-Mail und sozialer Medien.

Die Zaraffel sind...

Mirona C.

In Transylvania and Potsdam I find myself at home. I enjoy being befallen (vertically) by excellent literature, art and/or theory. Often, my slightly pessimistic mood is being improved by rings and earrings out of or with natural stones. If I feel the need to escape, then my preferred choices are the mountains. Or Zaraffel. Here I can write, paint or draw freely through my personal lens. And have refreshing exchanges of ideas, as well as valuable conversations within a colourful group, through which I can develop further. And stay critical.

Stella Chachali

I spend my days between Athens and Potsdam, image and text, reality and dream, to be or not to be. I enjoy reading and writing words, viewing and drawing images, listening and singing notes. With eyes practiced in beauty, I am learning to communicate better with you, to hug you in a warmer way and to struggle for you or next to you with more passion. Small as a child, with colourful clothes, I am a member of Zaraffel. As Zaraffel, I try to surpass semiotic borders and to develop polyphonic correspondences, taking part in a magnificent collage of ideas and signs.

Chen-Rui

Nein, einen Spitznamen habe ich nicht, und ja, Chen-Rui ist mein
Vorname. Was ich so mache? Naja, dies, das, Dinge halt. Auf Arbeit geht
es immer sehr hektisch zu. Daher mag ich es zu Hause eher ruhig. Und
gemütlich. Als ich vor einigen Jahren an einem Flughafenschalter, direkt
vor meiner Nase, ein herrenloses Exemplar von „Die Entdeckung der
Langsamkeit" fand, hielt ich es für Schicksal – ein Buch über John
Franklin, der beim Ballspielen so langsam war, dass er nur zum
Leinehalten taugte, der immer wieder getäuscht wird von den plumpen
Streichen der Hühner, ein Außenseiter, der aber in seiner Langsamkeit
sich in Bedächtigkeit übt und ein Auge fürs Detail entwickelt.

Georgios Dagkakis

Hey there! My name is *Γιώργος*; this is how it is written in Greek and
it sounds like Yioryos; kind of at least. I can try to pronounce it to you
next time we meet, but feel free to call me George, Georges, Georg – I
respond to all of these, and more. In the mornings, I work in front of a
PC, and at nights I sometimes write on one; other times I read, yet that
is most often on paper (coming from a generation that cannot feel
reading on screen as relaxing) but also on the computer, mostly when
the words come from friends, to which I frequently reply.

Erik Eising

Im Osten der Republik aufgewachsen und im Westen großgewachsen, wohne ich seit über zehn Jahren im Raum Berlin. Ich esse gern Toastbrot mit Leberwurst und Kartoffeln mit Quark. Außerdem bin ich der Herausgeber des Zaraffel-Magazins, für welches ich kurze, mittlere und längere Texte schreibe und redigiere. Dabei sind mir viele Dinge wichtig, doch eines treibt mich besonders an, nämlich dem Neuen zu begegnen – weil ich weiter wachsen will. Man weiß doch nichts von sich, wenn man das Andere nicht kennt, oder was sagst Du? Wenn wir uns das nächste Mal treffen, dann sag mir doch, was Dir wichtig ist; ich bin schon gespannt.

Tim Redfern

I grew up in Melbourne, but fate brought me unexpectedly to Berlin. Now I live between books, a screen, red wine, and my nostalgia for the forests and fresh air of Toolangi and the Dandenongs. I get my kicks from delving deep into literary-politico-theological worlds and then rearranging their patterns anew on the page. I see the world as text, at once both human and divine, written but still open for rewriting; fixed and yet free to be endlessly remade. As a contributor to Zaraffel, I am excited to be part of a literary project that reflects both diversity and relationality.

Mark Farrier

Here goes a try to describe this mischung melange i carry: Former san fran/nyc resident… AKA Chomps/Chops/Free Lunch/Manx/etc… Anarcho-punk queer protester burner witch artist poet and theory student… Ten years ago disembarked into this ever fractured swirl of the berlin-o-sphere. I'm very happy to join this great group of z people willing and loving to trance-scribe these worlds of experiences into such a beautiful journal!

WAS BISHER GESCHAH...

(von Erik Eising)

Im Anlauf zur Veröffentlichung dieser fünfte Ausgabe des Zaraffel-Magazins nahmen unsere drei hinzugewachsenen jungen Mitglieder die Hauptrolle ein. Das zeichnet sich auch in den diesmal vorgestellten Arbeiten ab: Von Vorfreude, Sehnsucht und Liebe handeln sie einerseits, und andererseits von Erinnerungen aus eigenen Kindertagen, die anlässlich solch existenzieller Ereignisse aus unbewussten Tiefen heraustauchen. Unsere Kinder sind wohlauf und erfinden sich jeden Tag ihre Welt ein Stückchen weiter (und ihre Eltern helfen ihnen hier und dort). Und genau so lade ich euch ein, auch Zaraffel zu lesen: Mit jungen Augen, die neue Routen entdecken, anstatt die gewohnten zu suchen. Kommt also an Bord und schwebt mit uns durch immer wieder unentdeckten Raum… Leinen los!

Neben den drei jüngsten Zaraffeln dürfen wir einen neuen dienstältesten Poeten offiziell Willkommen heißen: *Mark Farrier* hat die Vision unterzeichnet und wird uns ab sofort als ständiges Mitglied begleiten. Seine Gedichte klangen bisher am lautesten aus dem Taubenschlag heraus, von wo diesmal gleich vier Gäste einen zum Besten geben.

Besonderen Dank gilt dabei *blumenleere*, in dessen Literaturmagazin „Zur Philosophie des Schenkens" in diesem Jahr schon ein Beitrag von mir erscheinen konnte. Wo ihr das bekommen könnt, erfahrt ihr im Taubenschlag.

Wir haben lange gebraucht, ihn dran zu bekommen, doch diesmal ist es soweit: Im Schlafittchen geht es endlich einmal *Georgios Dagkakis* an den Kragen, dessen Katalog an Kurzgeschichten auch in dieser Ausgabe wieder ein Glanzstück hinzugefügt wird. In "The Times and Life of Brian Little" biographiert er ein vergessenes Genie der Musikgeschichte, dessen Fähigkeiten so unglaublich waren, dass er für sein trauriges Schicksal selbst auf den Teufel nicht angewiesen war.

Zusammen mit Stella Chachali führt er am Ende des Magazins ein eher ungewöhnliches Interview. Zwei Protagonisten aus vergangenen Ausgaben kommen ins Gespräch und scheinen dabei erstaunlich gut informiert über ihren Zustand zu sein…

Abschließend sei erwähnt, dass einige Änderungen in der Präsentation des Magazins vorgenommen worden sind, die dabei helfen sollen, die Namen der entsprechenden Autorinnen und Autoren leichter zu finden sowie die Referenztexte im Echolot besser ausfindig zu machen. Außerdem werden die Texte in verändertem Typ dargestellt, was der leichteren Lektüre dienlich sein soll.

All that being said, wünsche ich euch im Namen der Zaraffel viel Vergnügen mit der fünften Ausgabe. *Bon voyage, καλό ταξίδι*! Wir sehen uns hoffentlich zur nächsten Lesung.

Inhalt

KRITZELEIEN — 17

Unter dieser Rubrik stellen die Zaraffel ihre Haupttexte vor.

Zaraffels Vision

Du wirst dich gefragt haben, was wir damit meinen und wir werden Dir geantwortet haben, Du müsstest nur in Dich hinein gehört haben. Tausend Fragen oder ein paar weniger, selten zählt mal einer nach. Seltener noch ist eine dabei, die Dich wahrhaftig angeht. Der ganze verdammte Rest liegt sanft begraben; unterm Flickenteppich der Beruhigungsunterhaltung liegen betäubte Zweifel gekehrt neben Staubwolken, Reihe für Reihe, als wäre weiter nichts los. So ist unser Leben, reden wir uns ein und hoffen dabei doch zu oft, wir mögen es uns selbst geglaubt haben. Wir irren, weil wir wandeln. Als es der ahnungsvollen Zweifel zu viele wurden, begann sich etwas zu regen in uns. Als Bewegung zunächst ziellos, richtete Zaraffel sich zeitig auf. Dies Heft, das Du in Händen hältst, wird die Verkörperung unserer Vision gewesen sein.

Ob es der Mühe wert gewesen sein wird? Die Tätigkeit des anderen zu verstehen, unter größtmöglichen Anstrengungen zu bezeigen, was denjenigen, der mit mir in Kontakt tritt, angeht, was ihn bewegt, was ihn ausmacht: das ist es, was sich für Zaraffel wahrhaftig anfühlt. Unsere Vision ist daher die der Korrespondenz und jeder, der sie teilt, ist Teil von Zaraffel. Ob es sinnvoll gewesen sein wird? Na unbedingt, es wird sogar nichts als Sinn gewesen sein. Scheinbar ist gerade alles zu haben, wenn nicht zum Sonderpreis, dann doch wenigstens mit überaus geringem Aufwand erhältlich. Ob Charisma, Charakter, Kreativität; Wissen wurde zu Information, und damit erwerbbares Gut; Anstrengung und jegliche vorangegangene Arbeit scheinbar überwunden. Der genusssüchtige Optimismus kauft sich frei von Mühe, während er sich weiterhin einredet, jede Zukunft sei möglich, nur noch nicht eingelöst. Bloß, die Zukunft wird kein verwerteter Gutschein gewesen sein. Es benötigt Zeit, Arbeit und Strebsamkeit – Hingabe – um hinnehmbare Ergebnisse zu erzielen und sowohl das, was hinter dem Ereignis steckt als auch das, was ihm vorausgeht, ist oft deutlich bemerkenswerter.

Das einst zwingende Spiel, der eingleisige Humor, ist also ernst geworden: Nur weil neue Antworten auf alte Fragen gefunden wurden, machte sie das nicht weniger fadenscheinig. Auch das Neue hat ein Recht darauf, kritisiert zu werden, und Recht ist notwendig, da ansonsten sich die längst verschwommenen Konturen relationsloser Kategorien wie „gut" und „böse" wieder einschärfen würden. Wir sehen niemanden mehr, der darüber ein für alle Mal urteilen könnte: Allein im anhaltenden

You will have been asking yourself what this means, and we will have been answering: you just needed to listen to your own inner voice. A thousand questions – give or take a few – will have been running through your mind. You will have rarely been keeping track. Rarer still might one of these questions have truly concerned you.

The whole bloody rest has gently been buried, your doubts lying numb beneath a frayed rug of sedative entertainment, swept between piles of dust, as if nothing was really happening. That's how life is, we tell ourselves, hoping all too much that we just might believe it. We stray as we wander. Once the ominous doubts became too many, something within us began to stir. In due time emerged a movement, directionless at first: Zaraffel. The printed volume that now rests in your hands will have been the embodiment of our vision.

Will it have been worth the effort? To comprehend the work of another; to understand, even with the greatest possible effort, those who reach out to us; understanding what concerns them, what moves them, what they stand for – that is what feels truthful for Zaraffel. Our vision is thus a vision of correspondence, and those who share it deserve their share in Zaraffel. Will it have been meaningful? Without a doubt. It will, in fact, have been nothing but meaning.

These days it seems that anything can be accomplished without the slightest effort, and if not, it is for sale. Whether charisma, character, or creativity, it doesn't matter; knowledge has collapsed into mere information, and, as such, become a commodity. Honest endeavour and labour seem superseded. Hedonistic optimism buys its way out of pain, all the while believing that any future is possible if it can only be cashed-in on. The future, however, will not have been a coupon.

It takes time, labour and ambition – in a word, commitment – to achieve satisfactory results. Both what is behind the event as well as what precedes it, is more than meets the eye. The once compelling game, a one-sided humour, became serious: just because new answers were found to old questions does not mean they are less threadbare.

Austausch kann es noch gelingen, zwischen den Aporien des Lebens zu vermitteln.

Gott war nur mal Kippen holen, doch kam nie mehr zurück. Sein Abgang, wenn auch von schwachen Geistern und Kindsköpfen anderer Gesinnung spöttisch begrüßt, war keineswegs versuchshalber oder auf Probe. Nietzsche vermisste ihn schrecklicher als viele nach ihm. Das Ziel, die zweckmäßige Handlung indes, war auserkoren worden, diesen Verlust zu kompensieren. Entwicklung und Fortschritt, ursprünglich noch von Gottes Gnaden, sollten nun ihren einstigen Gönner ersetzen; ein Fehlentwurf. Übrig blieb allein das Ziel um seiner selbst willen – die Bedeutung solch gestalteter Industrie ist heute so hohl wie das Zeichen, dem sie entsprungen war. Wie so manches unter den Teppich gekehrt wird, wurden dabei innere Prozesse der obsessiv verfolgten Entwicklung zu Unrecht vernachlässigt.

Nun müssen wir doch feststellen, dass sich unsere Erkenntnis derselben Illusion des Untergangs verdankt. Philosophen schrieben *„causa causae est causa effectus"* und meinten damit, selbst unser Scheitern wäre nicht grundlos. Wir lassen es erst gar nicht darauf ankommen und werden noch heute tätig. Warum, fragst du dich? Zaraffel wartet nicht in lethargischer Ewigkeit, im Komfort der glattkonstruierten Plastewelten des Digitalen. Wir müssen es tun, weil Ihr es nicht macht. Wir fühlen es auf unseren Schultern; auf unseren Armen und Beinen, auf unserer Generation lasten Generationen von Schulden, manche eingelöst und wieder andere nicht. Das meiste ist nicht Dein Problem, doch sei herzlich eingeladen, hier zu halten, die Reisekoffer stehen zu lassen und den Flug mit uns zu verpassen, sobald Du in dieser Wunderkammer voller Kuriosa einen Ansporn dazu gefunden hast. Lass mich versuchen, Dir in der Zwischenzeit aufzuzeigen, weshalb wir uns dafür verantwortlich fühlen wollen. Diese Verantwortung, welche sich für uns aus der Notwendigkeit heraus ergab, werden wir gemeinsam übernommen haben.

Mit Gott starb sowohl der Anspruch auf Moral als auch das perfekte Motto, ferner wurde die Wahrheit an sich verdächtig. An sich selbst zu denken ist als Handlung intellektuell oft notwendig und moralisch indifferent; Gemeinschaft aber entsteht nur dann, wenn für das Wesen ihrer Mitglieder gesorgt würde. Zaraffel wird denen Trost ($\pi\alpha\rho\alpha\mu\acute{v}\theta\iota$) gespendet haben, die Mitleid als einzige Triebfeder moralischen Handelns begriffen haben.

Mitleid, moderner: Empathie, ist wie jedes Wort nur Träger derjenigen Botschaft, die sein Empfänger in der Lage ist herauszulesen.

Even that which is new must be criticized; this is necessary, in fact, lest such shapeless categories as "good" and "evil" be again allowed to sharpen their edges. We no longer recognise anyone who can judge these matters once and for all. Solely in continuous correspondence lies a chance to mediate between the aporia of life.

God went out for a pack of cigarettes and never came back. His departure, even if mockingly welcomed by naïve loons and dubious minds, was anything but probationary. Nietzsche missed God dreadfully, more so than many who came after him. Compensating for that loss became, subsequently, the preeminent goal. Development and progress, once made possible by the grace of God, were to replace their former patron. A design fault. What was left over, then? Nothing but progress for progress' sake; the goal of merely having a goal. Today the significance of this endeavour remains as empty as the sign from which it first emerged. As so much is swept under the rug, the inner processes of this obsessively pursued development have been unfairly neglected. Alas, this insight we owe to the same illusion of demise.

Philosophers used to write *"causa causae est causa effectus"*, whereby they meant that even our failure would not have been without reason. We do not want to take our chances, and so we choose to act immediately. Why, you ask? Because Zaraffel cannot wait in lethargic eternity, in the comfort of the constructed, plastic worlds of the digital. We have to act, because others do not. We sense a weight upon our shoulders, upon our arms and legs. Our generation's shoulders carry generations' worth of burdens, some already redeemed, others not.

Most of it is not your problem, but feel free to stay here, leave your baggage where it stands, and miss your flight together with us and allow something in this cabinet of curiosities to catch your eye. In the meantime, let us explain why it is that we want to feel responsible. This responsibility, which for us has arisen out of necessity, is one we will have been assuming together.

With God died not only the entitlement of morality but also the "perfect motto"; moreover, truth itself became suspicious. To care about one's own well-being is intellectually often necessary; morally, it is indifferent.

Unmittelbar geäußertes Mitleid wirkt deshalb oft künstlich, weil es selbst nichts mehr fühlt; diejenige Sprache, die man allgemein für eindeutig hielt, war längst umgewertet worden in ihr ironisch verzerrtes Gegenteil. Das natürliche Abbild des Mitleids, des sich Identifizierens, ist darum im Mittelbaren statt im Unmittelbaren zu suchen – im Text; doch mehr noch als die unmittelbare Kommunikation, steht die mittelbare als Vehikel zur Ausräumung falscher Eindeutigkeiten allein auf weiter Flur.

Wo konventionelle Sprache ebenso wie *computer-mediated-communication* zum aneinandergereihten Geschäftsverkehr belanglosester Information verkommen ist, verlautet das verdichtete Wort die Überwindung von Schluchten zwischen den einzelnen. Uneindeutigkeit auszuhalten ist der unumstößliche Gegenpol zur Fixierungssucht von Bedeutung in unserer immer komplexer werdenden Geschichte. Der Sinn, nach welchem wir streben, fällt nicht einfach aus seinen Buchstaben heraus, sondern muss innerhalb dessen, was er bedeutet, am äußersten Rand seiner Halbwertszeit, immer aufs Neue empfunden werden. Wir sind nicht naiv genug zu glauben, dieses sei ein konventionelles Problem, welches sich technisch lösen ließe.
Zaraffels responsiver Charakter verdingt sich seiner uneindeutigen Vielfalt. In einer erneuerten Literatur muss dieser Vision nach das Ineinanderspielen von Form und Funktion, ihrer historischen Entwicklungen nachspürend, bezeugt sein. Wo immer Distanzen zwischen Lesen und Schreiben überwunden werden, kommen wir zusammen, improvisieren und spielen wir. Unter solcher Definition entgeht auch dieses gedruckte Heft der Staubwüste der Beliebigkeit, allein da es sich ob seiner Materialität nicht in beliebigen Händen befinden kann; es spricht nur zu Dir und doch mit allen, die es lesen; mit allen, die es verstehen lernen wollen. Zaraffel wird sich seinem ambigen Sinn verschrieben haben.

Zaraffel hat keinen monetären Profit im Sinn, und doch verschenken wir nichts. Wir bieten nichts, das diejenigen leeren Symbole, denen wir uns tagtäglich ausgesetzt wissen, abpaust. Druckpreis und Almosen (ἐλεημοσύνη) sind das Signum dieser einzigen Politik, der wir uns qua Produkt anzubiedern bereit zeigen. Wer nichts hat, soll nehmen dürfen und wer geben will, der gibt. Es ist die Hoffnung auf das Kommende in positive Warenlogik übersetzt. Was wir euch nicht verkaufen, ist die Illusion, wir könnten uns die Druckkosten aus den Rippen scheuern.

Community, however, emerges only when we become concerned for the very being of the Other. Zaraffel will have been offering comfort (παραμύθι) to those who understood compassion as the sole driving force of moral action.

Compassion. Or, to put it in more modern language: Empathy. Like all words, it transmits only the message its receiver is able to discern. Empathy, when expressed directly and without mediation, feels often artificial because it itself feels nothing anymore; the very same language once believed to be unambiguous has long since been transvalued into its ironically distorted opposite. Self-identification, compassion's natural image, thus has to be sought in the mediate rather than the immediate – in text, where, lonelier than immediate communication, mediate communication ploughs its own furrow.

Whereas both conventional language as well as computer-mediated communication have been corrupted into the commercial traffic of utterly trivial information, the poeticised word makes known the need to cultivate these fields anew. To tolerate ambiguity is the undeniable antipole to the obsessive specification of meaning in our history that, minute by minute, becomes ever more complex. The purpose we strive for does not just fall out of its letters but requires that its meaning be felt over and over again, up to the very limits of its half-life period. We are not so naïve as to believe this is a conventional problem that could be solved technologically.

Zaraffel's responsive character serves its ambiguous diversity. In a renewed literature that follows this vision, the intertwinement of its form and function must be attested to by tracing their historical development. Wherever the distance between reading and writing can be overcome, we come together, we improvise, and we play.

According to this definition, even this printed volume escapes the desert of arbitrariness, as it cannot rest in arbitrary hands. It speaks to you only, and yet to everyone that reads it; to everyone who wishes to learn to understand it. Zaraffel will have thus devoted itself to its ambiguous purpose.

Zaraffel does not have monetary motives, yet we have no gift to give. We offer nothing that retraces those empty symbols to which we are exposed daily. Printing costs plus alms (ἐλεημοσύνη) are the signs of this single policy to which we, *qua product*, subscribe to.

Nicht allein darum wird man Zaraffel Opportunismus vorgeworfen haben. Der privilegierten Bürde unserer Handlungsfreiheit verpflichtet, belächeln wir diese Kritik herzlichst. Wir handeln heterogen, aus unterschiedlichsten Hintergründen heraus spinnen wir unsere Fäden, verweben unterschiedlichste Themen zu unterschiedlichsten Texten und Textsorten – ausschließlich bisher unveröffentlichtes Material. Dabei wird die Multiplizität unserer Einflüsse zwar von der Oberfläche unserer unterschiedlichen Erfahrungen her entworfen, gleichwohl bezeichnet der Mittelpunkt ihrer Schnittmenge jenen Grund, dessen Tiefe es gilt unter Aufwendung der größten Vorsicht zu ermessen, allmählich, rücksichtsvoll, *lentement*. Unsere gemeinsamen Koordinaten zu erkunden, wird unser Ziel gewesen sein, für dessen Umsetzung wir uns die Hilfe vieler Ähnlich-, Anders- und Weiterdenkenden ausrechnen.

Noch einmal: Was hier geschieht, erscheint uns notwendig; wir suchen, finden, haben alles und nichts. Wir wollen uns nicht politischen Richtungen oder Minderheitsdiskursen affiliieren, gleichzeitig sehen wir keinen Anlass darin, unsere historisch gewachsene Bedingtheit zu bestreiten. Privilegiert sein heißt, ein Problem ignorieren zu können. Zu jeder Tageszeit werden wir das „sowohl als auch" dem „entweder oder" vorziehen. Zaraffel ist kein Vektor, kein Pfeil, der, einmal abgefeuert, nie von seiner Bahn abkommt. An einem schönen Bahnhof auszusteigen, zu verweilen, zu lauschen, eine Kleinigkeit zu verstehen ist Zaraffel; ist: zu gleichen Teilen Ziel und Haltestelle seiner Welt. Zaraffel wird sich als radikal widersinnig beschrieben haben.

~

Mirona C.,
Stella Chachali,
Georgios Dagkakis,
Chen-Rui Eising,
Erik Eising,
Mark Farrier
Tim Redfern

Those who have little shall be allowed to take; and those who wish to give, may give. This is the hope of what is to come, translated into the logic of commodities. We will not try to sell you the illusion we could conjure up our printing costs ourselves.

Not for this reason alone will Zaraffel have been accused of opportunism. Indebted to the privileged burden of our freedom, we greet this kind of criticism with heartfelt smiles.

We act heterogeneously, spinning our threads across diverse backgrounds, interweaving different topics in and throughout different texts and genres. Unpublished material only. In doing so, the multiplicity of our influences will be reflected from the surface of our diverse experiences, sketching at the same time the heart of their coordinates, whose depth we wish to gauge gradually, considerately, *lentement*. To explore our common coordinates will have been our goal, the realisation of which we entrust to the help of many who think alike, differently, and/or beyond.

Again: What happens right here seems necessary to us; we seek, find, and have everything and nothing. We do not want to affiliate ourselves to a particular political tendency, nor to a particular minority discourse; at the same time, we cannot deny our historical contingency. To be privileged means being in the position to ignore a problem. At all times, we will prefer the „Both/And" to the "Either/Or". Zaraffel is not a vector, an arrow that, once fired off, never strays from its course. Zaraffel is to hop off at a beautiful station, to listen, to understand a nuance. It is both the destination and waystation of its world. Zaraffel will have described itself as radically preposterous.

~

Mirona C.,
Stella Chachali,
Georgios Dagkakis,
Chen-Rui Eising,
Erik Eising,
Mark Farrier,
Tim Redfern

KRITZELEIEN

**Unter dieser Rubrik stellen die Zaraffel
ihre Haupttexte vor.**

Kritzeleien sind Gedichte, Essays, Kurzgeschichten, Comics,
Berichte oder ganz gemischte Formen – ein Allerlei aus
montagierten Arbeiten und Abbildungen spontaner
kreativer Prozesse, die auf ihre jeweilige Weise *Zaraffels
Vision* Audruck verleihen.

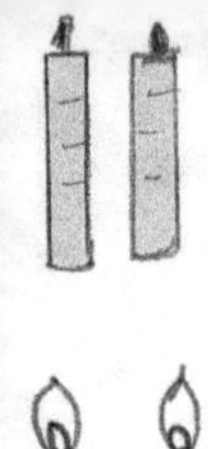
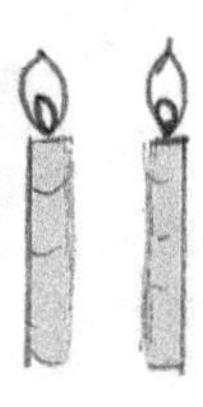
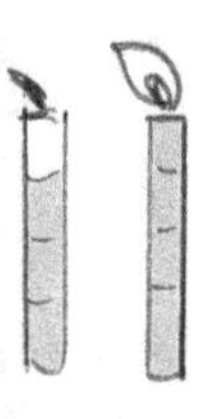

Liturgical Time / Of Feasts and Fasting

(by Tim Redfern)

"If our aim is to explore the farthest potentialities of being, we may well opt for the disorderliness and randomness of love. [...] The longed-for swoon is the salient feature not only of man's sensuality but also of the experience of the mystics."
— Georges Bataille, *Eroticism*

Advent

> "On a dark night
> Kindled in love and yearnings
> - oh, happy chance! -
> I went forth, unobserved
> My house being now at rest"
> — John of the Cross, *The Dark Night of the Soul*

It's four AM, but don't go yet
Lay here a while and talk with me
as I imagine touching your hair
and tracing my hand
down your neck
over your shoulders
across your body's tender landscape.

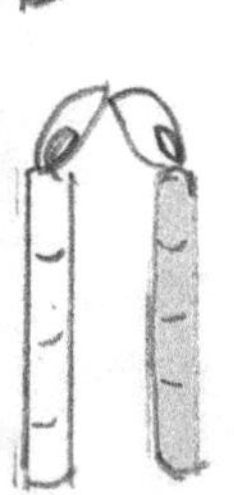

The night is still young, like us
as we sit alone upon the field
Two boys, lips stained with red wine
Cigarette smoke in the balmy air.
My head dares upon your chest to rest
and awaits your hand to push away
but nervous seconds turn to minutes
and pass in graceful silence.
Your heartbeat echoes in my ear
And I could stay here forever
Tired, nervous, but in your warmth
Motion and time suspended.

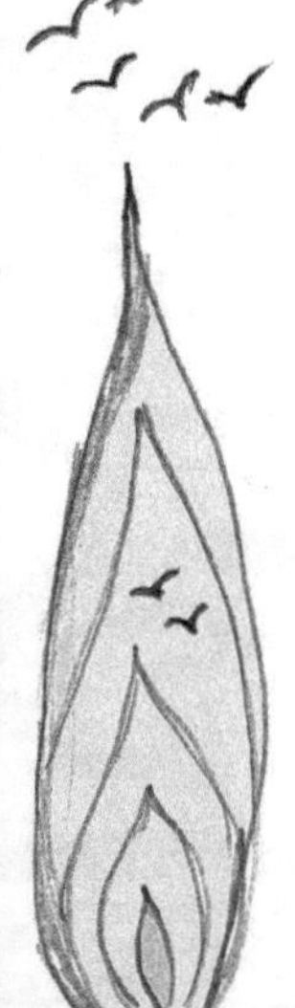

> "Upon my flowery breast,
> Kept wholly for himself alone
> There he stayed sleeping, and I caressed him
> And the fanning of the cedars made a breeze."

It's four AM, or perhaps just past
and beating hearts echo loudly
as speech and conversation fade.
Your nervous eyes connect with mine
and desire supplies a courage new:
I touch your neck
you draw me close
we both taste smoke and wine
angels keep guard around us
in our sanctuary in the fields.
shame and fear are left behind
as we touch the firmament
and dissolve all uncertainty.

"The breeze blew from the turret
As I parted his locks
With his gentle hand he wounded my neck
And caused all my senses to be suspended."

Time and world and rules all fade
as your fingers trace their way along my spine
into the small of my back
Every word and thought forgotten
and we dissolve and briefly die.
Eternity holds space for our transgression:
Your laughter and your voice
your breath on my face
my lips pressed on yours
I pray that this night might last forever
watched by sympathetic powers
And the smiling God of love.

"Oh, night that guided me,
Oh, night more lovely than the dawn
Oh, night that joined Beloved with the lover,
Lover transformed in the Beloved!"

Nativity

It was Christmas in Rome in the earliest hours as we walked back to our apartment after midnight Mass. The cool winter air was laden with the smells and sounds of festival. *Adeste Fideles* played from a loudspeaker at the square while tourists and locals and people under vows made their ways home through winding streets lit with Christmas lights, their soft white glow spreading gently upon the cobblestones beneath, shimmering in the windows of Roman arcades.

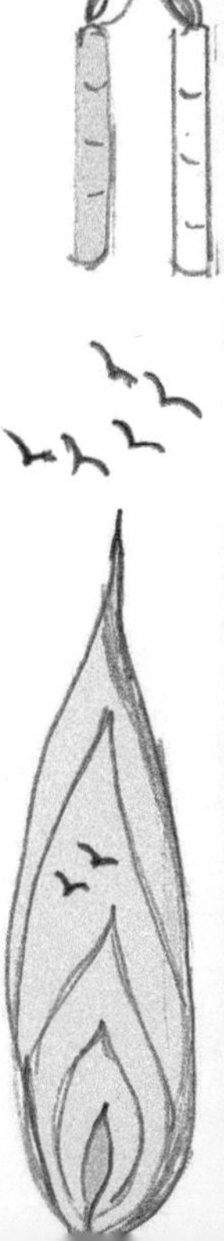

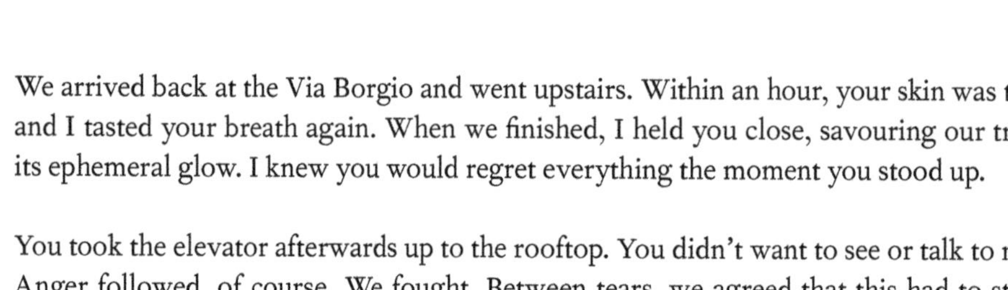

We arrived back at the Via Borgio and went upstairs. Within an hour, your skin was touching mine, and I tasted your breath again. When we finished, I held you close, savouring our transgression in its ephemeral glow. I knew you would regret everything the moment you stood up.

You took the elevator afterwards up to the rooftop. You didn't want to see or talk to me. Anger followed, of course. We fought. Between tears, we agreed that this had to stop. Loyalty to our baroque religion prevailed over our desire.

A few hours earlier, as the Solemnity of the Nativity began, we knelt in a vast, hallowed space that opened behind an inconspicuous church door in a Roman alleyway. Marble columns and a ceiling high as heaven ushered reverent awe into the air, tangible and thick as the thurible's fragrant smoke. The ancient choreography of the Roman rite unfolded as it had for a thousand years: full of mystery and desire. The choir's play of sound and silence suspended time and sense. Men and boys in lace, handsome and clean-shaven, processed back and forth before the altar, bowing, kneeling, ascending, descending.

Eventually the choir stopped and all fell silent, the stillness in that vast space interrupted only by the soft, metallic tinkling of the thurible chain. A bell chimed, and then again. We bowed our heads at the mystery upon the altar. We tapped our chests three times, reciting in a soft whisper "an ancient formula, newly learned": *Domine, non sum dignus, ut intres sub tectum meum, sed tantum dic verbo et sanabitur anima mea.*

> "Lord, I am not worthy
> Lord, I am not worthy,
> But speak the word only."

The ancient ritual approached its climax with the rite of communion. We came forward and knelt again. Two pilgrim boys, full of teenage lust and holy confusion, we closed our eyes and opened our mouths to receive upon our tongues another man's body in a way beyond sense and seeing. This was a ritual draped in the erotic, subliminally and symbolically enacting desires that dared not be thought or spoken, the desire for flesh translated as desire for heaven.

The priest arrived, resplendent in gold and white, a boy at his side. This older man – the *alter Christus* – placed the Body of Christ in our mouths, two boy-brides receiving the Bridegroom:

Corpus Domini nostri Iesu Christi custodiat animam tuam in vitam aeternam.

The thin, dry wafer touched my tongue. I tasted His substance and swallowed. It was a consummation without sensuality: enacted through words and signs, yet intimate and bodily beyond measure.

The Roman Mass is the original queer theatre. The ritual of that Christmas night was an act of eros, sublimated but alive, acted out by an ostensibly celibate man and boys who could barely suppress their own desires. The strictest rules of gender and sexuality were at once enforced and transgressed. Heavy vestments of lace and gold, thick clouds of fragrant smoke, concealed the male desire lurking beneath, a raw energy that had to be held back, sublimated, transformed at any cost into something pious and pure. A sacred economy of libido was transported into symbolism that still touched bodies and sent them into silent ecstasy.

Returning to my pew and kneeling, I begged: Lord, if it be possible, let this cup pass from me. It would be only a few more hours that night until that same eros overflowed its pious vessels, and the symbolic collapsed into the real.

The next morning we pretended that nothing had happened, until we landed in each other's arms and mouths again. And again. Boundaries crossed could not easily be redrawn.

You were bitter with me after that Christmas.
In love, and yet bitter.

For bitter it is, to trade the body's grace for the grace of self-denial.

Epiphany

I was in Brisbane, visiting a friend on a warm night when I realised my old life was over. I remember that evening, the tropical air, and the excited trepidation that filled me as I felt the past fall away, and with it the attachments of my former way of life. The new Daft Punk album had just been released and we listened to it on repeat as we sat in Chris's room, passing a joint. He spoke about his ex-girlfriend stealing his posters and band t-shirts as I drifted in and out, my attention shifting from him to the music and back again, the lyrics of 'Touch' echoing the quiet breakthrough that unfolded within me as I sat on the wooden floor.

It was that night in Brisbane that I finally gave myself permission to say: "enough." To move on. To leave behind a world I had inhabited for years, a world that had disciplined and punished the depths of my inner life and had driven a wedge between me and my own self.

It was an epiphany amidst soft French electropop and weed smoke, a turning-point in my life, an earthquake that unfolded quietly on the floor of a friend's apartment. The three of us laughed and chatted, the breeze sauntered in through open windows and cicadas filled the street outside with their evening song. I opened another beer, and the conversation flowed along, the others oblivious to the rupture that had just taken place. Oblivious that this gentle, unremarkable night would define my life from then on in terms of before and after.

Lent / The Great Fast

> "And although the soul is lifted up by such lofty experiences, he is still unsatisfied in his desire for more. He still thirsts for that with which he constantly filled himself to capacity, and he asks to attain as if he had never partaken. This truly is the vision of God: never to be satisfied in the desire to see Him. By looking at what he can see, one continually rekindles his desire to see more."
> – Gregory of Nyssa, *The Life of Moses*

We sit together in a dimly lit corner of the bar, the last customers refusing to leave despite all signs and signals from the staff. The barkeeper sweeps the floor as the manager starts to count the till, our continued presence a protest against the tyrannical passing of time. The night has passed too quickly. We have been together since the afternoon and have barely stopped talking, and even as the conversation slows and the silent pauses become more frequent, we are far from ready to say goodbye and go our separate ways.

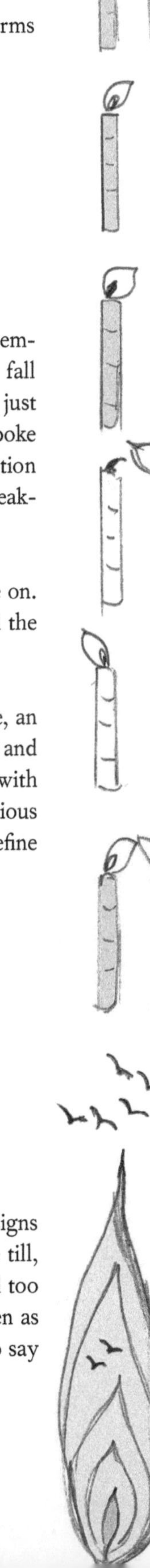

As I go to refill our glasses the barkeeper reminds me that the last round was called and done with half an hour ago. Coins ring in a tip jar and he is suddenly our friend. He fills our glasses and, with a knowing smile, says "you've got fifteen minutes."

It is futile. He could pour glass after generous glass all night: but with you, my cup is still never filled.

I can spend all day and night with you and still have barely started. I can see you every week and still feel like we will never spend enough time together. We can travel together, spend weeks together, drop our masks and guards together, cross every boundary together and still not have scratched the surface of how deeply I want to know you, possess you, lose myself in you. Behind your eyes is a universe; every word you utter a glimpse into a world I could fall into forever.

For this is truly the vision of you, never to be satisfied in the desire to see you, to talk to you, to hear another story, another thought, another sweet word pass your lips, another bright smile across your face, another gleaming in your dark eyes. There is no possession of you, only the image, the sand of you that slips between my fingers with every touch, every moment, every kiss. The light you burn cannot burn brightly enough; there is no satisfaction in infinite desire and I can only desire, desire, desire you and your body and your presence and everything you have to say and all that you are, more and more every time I see you, and even more when I do not see you. Even more when I do not see you. Even more and even more. It eats away at me like a hunger, a thirst, that will never be sated.

I could spend my life with you and it wouldn't be enough.

Passiontide

Sometimes I imagine what would have happened
    if you had not moved to Canada and
    if I had not gone back home.

I imagine we would have probably stayed together.

We would have spent more lazy summer mornings
    sitting upright in bed with the shutters open
    sunlight pouring into my room
    my arm around your shoulders
    holding you close
    as we read the news on our phones
    and the smell and taste of cheap espresso
    woke us up
    and drew us slowly
    out of each other's arms
    out of bed
    and into the day.

I would have tried not to smoke.

You would have put on my oversized red and orange jacket
        and looked so cute standing there in my room
        your legs bare
        your ass like a peach
        your feet delicate in those pink woollen socks.

Your messy hair would have glistened around your face
        catching beams of morning sunlight
        as you danced around my room
        to the music of that band
        that I pretended to like
        just because you liked them.

We would have stayed in your uncle's apartment in winter
        exploring the city in the fading sunlight hours
        soaking up the coarseness of a place
        where we both knew no one
        had no obligations
        no jobs
        no responsibilities.

We would have played again on that playground, like kids.
I would have taken more photos of us there
        smiling into the camera together
        pulling faces
        looking unbelievably happy.

I would have looked at those photos again years later
        and realised
        that my time with you was the first time
        I was ever really happy:
        not waiting for something else to happen
        or for life to change
        or for things to get better
        but just wanting everything to stay as it was
        just a bit longer…
        as long as possible.

I would wonder if I would ever feel that way again.

We would have trudged again through the snow,
        walking back from the city to your village
        because we always liked
        walking and talking together.
We would have talked about sex and sadness and philosophy
        and traded stories from our lives.
We would have only known each other a few months
        but still wanted to know everything about each other.

You would have been embarrassed to still be living with your parents.

You would have shown me your room in your family home
        the walls covered in poetry
        that you had handwritten and cut out,
        glued and taped to every surface.
You would have shown me that you also loved to write,
        that you had kept journals for years.

We would have gone walking in the forest nearby afterwards
        and had dinner in the village.
We would have had stayed up again all night
        in each other's arms
        entangled
        in each other's bodies.

Maybe you would have decided not to go to Canada after all.

I would not have found out that I was not ready to lose you.
I would not have felt like things were only just beginning.
We would not have gotten breakfast one last time
        in our favourite café, and
You would not have cried through the whole meal.
I would not have said a final goodbye to you at the station.
I would not have then realised how attached to you I had become.

I would not have missed you for years.

The Easter Triduum

I followed you to where the wind was still
Where silence hung about us like a shroud
And knocking at the gates of space and time
Sought refuge in your dark unknowing cloud

There sense and thought, suspended, lay asleep
As beams of sunlight spilt upon the floor
Your presence, beyond being, beyond mind
Hid playfully behind perception's doors

As darkness fell I called you by your name
And longed to disappear in your embrace
But to that other shore no path appeared
For in the dark I only saw her face

In shame I pushed her memory away
But time and time again she reappeared
Her graceful spectre stalked my every thought
An outlaw love my heart with madness seared

And so I fled the silence of that place
Not daring any more to look within
Where restless visions of desire danced
With bitter ghosts of who we could have been

From silent inner landscapes I withdrew
Abandoning all discourse with the One
To whom my restless heart had once aspired
And let life's troubles past me blindly run

Until one day your light broke in anew
On a quiet Easter Sunday morn:
A presence, once forgotten, smiling through
The face of a sweet child newly born

Fears and restless visions soon receded
And in the desert dark began to shine
Over barren land a light expanding:
An oceanic feeling, all sublime.

Ascension

> "Experience – according to Nietzsche, Blanchot, and Bataille – has rather the task of tearing
> the subject from itself in such a way that it is no longer the subject as such, or that it is
> completely 'other' than itself so that it may arrive at its annihilation, its dissociation. It is this
> de-subjectifying undertaking, the idea of a 'limit-experience' that tears the subject from
> itself."
> Michel Foucault, *Remarks on Marx: Conversations with Duccio Trombadori*

It was a cool, autumn evening, and the sun was setting slowly over the rooftops and streets of East
Melbourne. Standing inside an old, grey brick church, I watched as the light fell gently through
windows of stained glass, kaleidoscopic colours splashing over the painted icons that covered the
walls from floor to ceiling. I decided to sit for a while and wait as people slowly started arriving and
filling up the pews, oblivious to how strange the evening would become.

The service began unannounced. The side door of the iconostasis opened, and the deacon, a man
of about forty years with black hair and a beard, emerged in a black cassock. Seconds later, an
elderly priest followed him, an embroidered gold epitrachelion around his neck. In his hand he held
a golden censer hanging on three chains, each chain adorned with tiny bells that jingled softly with
his every step. The two men walked the perimeter of the nave, censing the icons on the walls as
they went, the soft, metallic clinking of bells and chains echoing gently as fragrant clouds of
incense filled the air.

The older man began to pray aloud in Arabic, softly at first, before his voice rose in volume and
pitch and flowed into a chromatic, musical chant. Standing in front of the iconostasis, the deacon
also began to chant a call-and-response litany with the choir, which by now had assembled around
a wooden kliros a few metres from where I sat. Each time, the bearded man's intercessions ended
on a long, sustained note that trailed off as the choir answered with a sonorous, deep *kyrie eleison*.

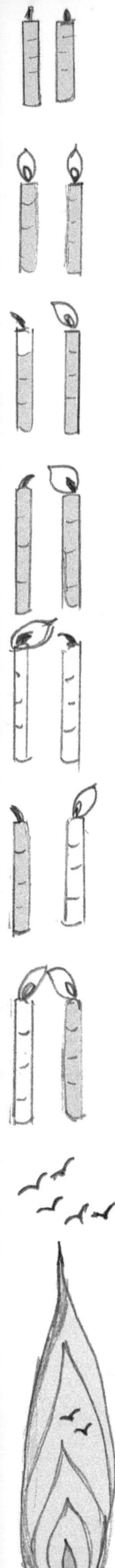

I understood nothing. I watched and listened, out of place and confused, an Anglo-Australian eighteen year-old in the midst of an ancient and foreign ceremony. Fire and colour danced as the evening light touched the iconostasis, rays of filtered sunset moving across its white, marble surface with each minute, the gold embossing lighting up like flame in the late amber glow. Ancient melodies in still more ancient tongues echoed with an eerie resonance, conjuring images of desert sands, of temples and fallen empires from ages past.

After a few minutes the call-and-response stopped, and silence filled the space again. In the minute that followed, I would experience something that I, for a long time, could neither describe nor understand, and which would haunt me forever afterwards.

The choir started again to sing, this time chanting only three times *alleluia*, slowly but with sustained vigour. Each individual syllable was drawn out over a journey of many notes, the melodies rising and falling like a rolling landscape. Dark, cloud-covered mountains opened into vistas of pure light and folded back into darkness again.

With the third *alleluia*, the pitch rose suddenly to a powerful height. The chorus of male voices bellowed out a melody sweet and nostalgic. Beautiful, unbearable, the eruptive force of the sound flooded the entire space. Pain and joy, fear and beauty, sweetness and sorrow: all flowed together, like a funeral dirge full of love for a lost child; like the ascent of a bird, flying higher and higher in a storm, breaking finally through the dark clouds to behold the bright sun above. The beauty and intensity of that sound overwhelmed my every sense and thought, blocking out everything else.

For perhaps ten seconds, I was gone. I went out of myself entirely, rising like a disembodied spirit above the choir, the kliros, the sanctuary, the world around me collapsing into a blinding light where nothing existed except that thunderous music. Every certainty unravelled; every doubt became certain reassurance. I dissolved, released from space and time, my entire being pulverised, flattened and obliviated by an agonising beauty that consumed everything in its overwhelming light.

I was terrified, and yet it was the most intense and ecstatic moment of my life until that point, unlike anything else I had ever felt. It was an experience that I would remember always, as clear as day, and never replicate, no matter how I tried with music, ritual, drugs, sex, or any other means to dissolve myself and reach such heights again. Nothing would ever compare to that beauty, so overwhelming that to stand in its presence was at once painful and ecstatic, an incomparable bliss, a taste of heaven, terrifying like an earthquake. That moment would haunt me like a bittersweet wound, never letting me go.

As quickly as it started, it was over. There I was again, a stranger in a strange place. Shaken, broken, dazed, I stood for the remainder of the service, no longer able to concentrate, no longer attempting to follow what was happening around me. I left afterwards without a word and took the tram home in silence.

Kleine Falten

(von Mirona C.)

Der Text hat mich,

Die Pflanze hat mich,

Eine kleine Falte sucht Ausdruck:

Ich schenke mich dem Unbekannten

pliu

pliaj

pliant

m-am repliat

Das Bild

Four New Poems

(by Mark Farrier)

The Juggernaut

Die Rose, welche hier dein äußres Auge sieht,
die hat von Ewigkeit in Gott also geblüht

[The rose, which your outer eye can see,
has blossomed in God for all eternity]

—Angelus Silesius

Can you hear the ancient mill wheel
Scraping against the firmament?
Try to hear it with your own body
Your *outer ear*, so to speak.
It is the ancient sound of time
Toned before any life here lived…

Vibrating forever
But also…
We can hear it!
Everybody in the universe can hear it!
Whether they have ears to hear or not.
It is the sound of space…

New Pome 23

Waking eye in the middle of night
Brightness invading the dark
Like 24 seven ivory blaze intruder

What is a pm anymore anyway
In this age of tawdry wired
Cheap fessions for
Brain's heart woe

Born in the sixties
Of a ward called x
Mosquito call
Woke me up
To tilt my ear

Toward still further kennings
Of trance induced Nevada wanderings
Yielding friction of search light
Yearnings for unbarred fangs of
Smoldering, blanketed, undying,
                everyday love

Habit

In German, *ohne denken*
"Without thinking"
The thorn we wear
In the vale of the record

But isn't thinking itself
Our greatest habit?

For what do we do
Without thinking?

One of us put forth
Many years ago
That thinking is the only vehicle
That can take you to the 'I am',
the *sum* of our *cogito*

Yet is it not rather
That we get there
Through the great
      without,
The within and wherefore and whereto,
      the space between
That carries all our life pulses,
All our throbbings of
      ex-perience

Wearing this habit
Of no one-ery,
Finding the otherness —
The im-possibili-tense —
      That carries us through

Line Age

On a Train
from way out west
That's how I got here

Passing generations going
The other direction

An unmigration, a Flee
A radio question

Without a filter
All tests a hazing
Of sweaty brows
We have been borne

A slant Movement
A kind of falling
Back in line

Our ancestors,
Rays of Light

The Life and Times of Brian Little

(by Georgios Dagkakis)

For most people the name Brian Little may sound vaguely familiar. They might say it *rings a bell*, which they'd find a suitable expression, since in their memory the name is somehow associated with music. Fewer may speak about a legendary musician, a huge, yet lost talent, which left behind some good music and many extravagant anecdotes. Of course there are also many who will say that they have never once heard this name in their lives. The one certain fact is that all of the above have listened to music of Brian Little several times, have hummed it, have woken up with one of his tunes stuck in their heads, have fallen in love with their darling dancing to one of his pieces or even had one of his melodies played at their funeral.

When talking about the story of Brian, it is not always easy to discriminate between the myth and the reality. We know that Brian was born in New Orleans on the second of February in the year 1945. The legend goes that he showed his musical talent at the earliest possible moment, when he was an embryo. During the fourth month of the pregnancy he started kicking in a steady rhythm of 4/4, but very soon he started experimenting with 5/4 and 9/8 and later the time signatures became so complicated that it would be hard even for the music theorist to count them. All this may be an exaggeration; what is sure is that his mother had a terrible pregnancy and she died just right after giving birth from complications due to arrhythmia.

Brian grew up with his father, John Little, who was of British origin and often claimed that he was a direct descendant of Robin Hood's partner with the same (but in reverse) name. He was an unsuccessful musician and realised very early the special talents of his son, which made him think he could become a new Leopold Mozart. He believed that his son could fulfil the dreams that he himself never managed to follow and, most importantly, earn him a lot of money. Being violent by nature, he pursued his plan by locking the boy—beginning when he was two years old—inside his room and forcing him to study music 20 hours a day. No matter what, the boy showed an exceptional appetite for learning and very soon became a proficient piano player and shortly after that mastered several other instruments.

At the age of seven, Brian's father started taking him to the bars he used to play at himself, some of the most dangerous places in the district, where nevertheless the regulars stood in awe before the talent of the young boy. He soon became popular in those places and the owners paid a fair amount for his appearances, so his father decided to take him out of school to gain the biggest possible advantage. Brian did not care, he did not have any friends in school anyway; he looked funny and the other boys bullied him and called him a "frog" (though some claim this was due to his smell). He started feeling at home in the ambiance of smoke and alcohol; it was a better atmosphere than home actually. Now that his father had some money, his drinking problem got worse, making him even more violent. At the age of 13, after a big fight, during which John Little almost killed his son, Brian fled home.

He continued playing in bars and making a living of his own. In one of these appearances he was discovered by an agent named Stuart Rich. Rich, who was also an addicted gambler, felt like he was holding a flush royal. He booked more shows for Brian, in bigger and tidier places and the following year he recorded his first album entitled "I'm Just a Little Little", which consisted of 11 original pieces, performed by Brian on the piano, with the total duration of 34 minutes. The story is that Brian had composed 10 songs, but Rich could only afford to book the studio for 20 minutes so he suggested to Brian to pick half of them. However, the little genius decided to play the songs at double speed and one octave higher than what they were supposed to be. Then they played the recording at half rotations and it sounded just perfect. So he managed to record 34 minutes of music within 17 minutes; having another 3 minutes, he improvised one more tune called "We have a Little time left", which according to music historians is the first time ever that the term "bonus track" was used.

"I'm just a little Little" was released in 1958 and sold thousands of copies even though it had almost zero publicity. For sure it had a good money turnover taking into account that it was produced at almost zero cost. However, Stuart Rich made off with the profits and Brian never saw him again. At this point in time, the teenage musician, now more than 14 years old, started a long and lonely wandering across the United States that lasted almost 3 years. He travelled from city to city, playing in bars and small music stages, gathering money and experiences. According to legend, it was during this *flânerie* that he came upon the notorious crossroads - the place where many successful musicians like Robert Johnson or Jimi Hendrix supposedly sold their souls to the devil, in order to become proficient in music. Brian did meet the fallen angel and the negotiations were long and intense; you see, the young musician did not lack anything regarding his talents on any instrument or with music in general. Finally, it was the devil that had to sell his soul to Brian.

In July of 1962 he felt that he had enough of his nomadic life and decided to come back to recording his own music. He signed a deal with Astral Daze Records, the famous company that believed in his talent. They gathered an impressive group of talented musicians to accompany him because it was getting increasingly hard to find people that could follow him in his exceedingly complex musical paths. "Brianorama" was released by the end of the year and it is considered by many to be Little's greatest record. It contains 7 long pieces that gracefully combine jazz with symphonic music with delta blues with oriental harmonies. Allegedly, Frank Zappa was so impressed when he first heard "Brianorama" that he did "shit on his pants" and got the infamous photo of him in the toilet in order to immortalise the moment.

Of course, Brian's music was too complex to be widely popular, but the record release did make him quite popular among other artists. He settled in New York City and was much in demand at high class receptions, where he often played some music that left the attendants in awe. He started having occasional relationships with some of the most famous and desired female celebrities of the era. As we have already noted, he was not really good looking; nonetheless, many of those women have testified that they found this (otherwise boorish) modern Orpheus irresistible when he lured them in with his music.

After a few months he released the next album with the simple title "Two Little", which is also considered by some fans the greatest musical achievement of the 20th century. Of course, this is a bold statement that is not shared among the general populous. "Two Little" is an extremely complicated, continuous piece of music which is not easy to digest. It was so far ahead of its time that many musicologists, but also some oracles, have predicted it will take until 2067 for humanity to comprehend its full strength.

At that time, Brian's records and live appearances earned him enough money to go on living. The records were also profitable for the company, but not to the level that they felt his talent

could bring, so they soon started pressuring him to write more commercial stuff. It is rumoured that during that time he did give a couple of songs to other singers without being credited or keeping future royalties; those songs all became number one hits.

His personal interest was in discovering the next challenge, which he found when he accidentally heard that Beethoven wrote some of his greatest music while being completely deaf. (Even though Brian could memorise an entire symphony after hearing it for the first time and replay the part of each instrument, when it came to music history, he was surprisingly ignorant). Somehow he came up with the idea that Beethoven's achievement was something that he had to compete with. Causing great dissatisfaction to his record company, he spent the first quarter of 1964 locked in his apartment and wearing earplugs. The extravagantly titled output of this endeavour, *Ode to Deafness*, was the only symphonic work that he ever recorded under his own name. The piece was first performed live in September of the same year by the New York Philharmonic. As expected, its announcement caused a lot of complaints against the impertinent musician who was mocking the work of one the greatest musical figures of the past. The piece itself, although for the most part a perfectly serious symphonic work, contained near the end a seven-minute-long pause (or, to be more exact, 112 bars of pauses of different lengths, as one can see on the score) that outraged almost everyone in the audience; nonetheless, the 5 concluding chords that followed the pause were so genially placed that in the end everyone had to agree that they had experienced a masterpiece.

On the New Year's Eve of 1965, Brian attended a brilliant reception that was given by a major film production company in New York. He casually spent his time thinking about which of the numerous divas he would choose to attract and spend the turn of the year with. He did take care to spend some time on the piano early on at the event (even though, when he was first asked to, he courteously denied) so he was confident that he had already cast the net and he would get to the fish soon. He was drinking his cocktail and having a chit-chat with Marlon Brando when he saw Emily for the first time. Emily Taylor was an artist and also the sister of the famous fashion icon Joan Taylor; Emily was standing a little further away enjoying a drink with her sister. Even though Joan was one of the most desirable women of the time, Brian did not notice her at all; his attention was entirely focused on Emily: "that's the one," he thought. He approached the girls with the air of confidence of a man who was used to being successful with women.

"Hello ladies, my name is Brian"

"Hello Brian," it was Joan that responded. "I am Joan Taylor," she said, giving the impression of repeating something that the interlocutor should already know. "And this here is my sister Emily," she showed Emily and then turned to her: "Emily, Brian is the guy that I told you about who gave a marvellous performance on the piano about an hour ago".

"Hum, so you were not here when I played?" he asked a bit uneasily. He did not fancy having to play again in order to captivate her. For an instant he selfishly thought that it would be pointless, there were so many other women there: he should turn somewhere else.

"No, she was here," it was Joan again that spoke. "It's just that she didn't listen to you. My sister has completely lost her hearing since she was a child," she explained.

"When you talk to me please make sure that I can see your mouth so I can make out what you say," remarked Emily. He noticed that, despite being deaf, she had a charming voice; for some

reason it sounded to him like crystal clear flowing water running into a small well. "I have read about your impressive work though. The other day I was reading in the newspaper about 'Ode to Deafness'"; she had uttered the title in a mockingly pompous manner. Many people in my condition considered it quite insulting, but I kind of found it charming," she said with a smile.

Brian found her smile also charming. This was a completely new situation for him. He was accustomed to winning over every woman easily; he just had to find an instrument and start cuddling her ears. Even without an instrument, he would find something around to make the needed musical show; he was very creative in this. However, right now he felt like a hairless Samson; he was perfectly aware that he had no other strong point: he was not good looking, he was awful with words and his behaviour was always problematic. In all of his previous relationships, he acted from start to finish like a jerk, knowing that everything could be instantly forgiven by playing some small magical melody.

While he was talking to the Taylor sisters, he could feel that Joan was fascinated by him. She had the same hungry eyes that he had seen in many women that had heard him playing. Emily, on the other hand, was obviously untouched by such feelings. Sure, she was kind and friendly, she even seemed to enjoy his company, but nothing more than that. During the discussion Brian learnt that she dealt with many different kinds of art (apart from music, apparently) and she was a quite successful painter and poet. She had also made some surreal sculptures and designed some bizarre artistic clothes.

Of course Brian had minimal understanding about all the above. He never read poetry and reading in general was a tiring task for him. As for painting, he remembered the house with a garden that he painted a picture of when he was six years old; after his father was shown the picture by Brian, he tore it up and slapped him, telling him that he should practice music instead. Nonetheless he felt that somehow Emily was different than the other artists he had encountered before. He could not put it into words, but she felt more "true". Generally, she felt truer than any-thing else he had met in his life so far. He himself tried to remain as untrue as possible, hiding his brutal manners and his utter ignorance regarding everything intellectual apart from his unique relationship with music. Strangely enough he did not do so badly; it was also for his benefit that apparently Joan was eager to meet him again, so he managed to keep their contact info and they promised to meet again soon.

When he woke up alone on the first morning of 1965, he had a strange feeling, a sour taste in his mouth that he attributed to alcohol and the fact that it was the first time in many years that he started his evening planning to find some girl to sleep with and then did not succeed. The strange feeling however was actually that of being in love, something that he was experiencing for the first and only time in his life. No-one will ever know if he fell in love with Emily or with the fact that she was inaccessible to him. Most likely it was a combination of the two.

The next time he met with the Taylor sisters he carefully avoided playing any music, so that he could get rid of Joan as fast as possible. She indeed became bored of him, even though she felt slightly jealous, understanding that Brian was more interested in her sister than in her. Emily on her side understood completely by now that Brian was totally unfamiliar with her kind of art, yet he tried hard to show a sincere interest. She found this funny, maybe even charming and somehow flattering.

In the spring of 1965, Brian finished his obligation for a series of concerts in the United States as quickly as possible. During that tour, which would be his last, his partners noticed a change in Brian's behaviour. It was the first time that he did not get drunk after (or during) the show; nor did he spend time with lady fans. On the contrary, he remained sober and returned to his room where he stayed alone till the next concert. After the tour he returned to New York with one thing on his mind: how to besiege Emily.

In June Emily presented some of her paintings in an exhibition. Brian visited it almost every day, watching the paintings for hours and, even though he did not understand anything about them, he genuinely loved them. Actually, he bought one; it was the most expensive, which he knew by checking the catalogue, but he told Emily that he had not noticed, he just thought it was the best. For some reason he believed that in this way he could show that he was capable of actually evaluating her art. Later, he attended a poetry reading with her. Some of the most promising talents of the new wave in the city, including Emily, would recite parts of their work. Brian listened patiently to the whole mass of words and tried to show that he could enjoy it. Later, he also wore his most polite smile, listening to some of the poets suggesting to him to adapt their work to music. For a moment he asked himself why Emily did not propose something similar, but apparently she did not care a lot for musical projects.

In the end, all his efforts paid off: he succeeded in making her accept an invitation at his place for dinner. He was excited! Although he kept having the annoying feeling that she was considering him just as a friend, he tried to discard it. For the first time in his life he did his best to make his house clean and tidy; he even changed the decor. He asked friends for advice and spent a lot of money to buy some paintings and hung them appropriately in the living room. Emily's painting was of course placed in the most prominent position. Furthermore, he bought many books and took special care to place them in his two new bookcases (he also bought two) so that they would look meaningfully arranged. He bought several bottles of expensive wine and made his first attempt to cook (he had also bought an oven).

At the moment that Emily was ringing his doorbell everything was ready. He felt an unprecedented excitement for the fact that he was welcoming a lady to his house. He sensed that, despite her engagement with modern art, Emily was deep inside a traditional girl, so he hoped that she would appreciate his old-school preparations; and he was actually right. The ambience he had setup was a success and, even though the food was barely edible, she found it charming that he did cook for her. They spoke about the painting on the wall and then about some of the books in the library. It was clear to her that he had practised the things he said and he did not avoid a couple of remarks that revealed his ignorance, yet she received the whole staged act as a compliment to her.

So the time did pass joyfully. Nonetheless, it did also pass fast and Brian feared it would soon be the time for her to say "Oh, it's time to go" or something similar. He wanted her; he madly craved to touch her; still, he did not know how. Normally in these cases he'd pick the first instrument, one of the many he had at home and it would be the notes coming from his hands and his heart that would do the first touching, until the ice was broken. Then, everything would be simpler. Some minutes on the piano, a small violin sonata, an improvisation on the guitar: each of these would be adequate. As far as he remembered, it was only once that nothing had worked and he had to go to the next room and return wearing only a tie and playing saxophone; that one did not fail. However, now all of his weapons were useless. This made him feel awkward, which in turn

made him fill his glass and empty it every few minutes. That, in combination with his empty stomach (he had to admit his food was awful), made his thinking cloudy. She was feeling his tension, so she tried to talk to him in a relaxed, easy-going manner in order to calm him, which on the contrary made him think that she was considering him just a friend. This was not true: she had growing feelings for him, but her feelings were like a delicate flower, they would need some time and proper conditions to blossom. On the other hand, Brian had no such experience with romance: he was under the delusion that he had to make her admire him as soon as possible.

"Do you want me to play some piano for you?" he said without even thinking. "Come!"

"I'd love to watch you…" she replied, trying to sound casual.

He was already seated with his hands hovering above the keys. Then he started. He played with an indescribable passion: all the feelings he repressed for so many months were now channeled by his magnificent talent and translated into a sublime melody. The notes were flowing with such strength that surely, if anyone was listening to them, they would be persuaded to abandon their own life and dedicate it to the performer. However, it was only the performer that was listening at that moment. Emily was unintentionally protected, like the shipmates of Ulysses, whose ears were filled with wax to prevent them being seduced by the sirens. If the sirens' song was even half as heavenly as the one Emily was *not* hearing, Ulysses would have found a way to bite and tear his ropes off. It was the greatest improvisation *never* heard!

Then Brian stopped playing and silence filled the room. Now they were listening to the same thing, apart from a cat meowing on the street, which only Brian heard. He turned to look at her with a yearning madness, with sweat dripping from his face. But no, there was no lust in her eyes, nor desire, not even excitement; only some pale mixture of sympathy and sadness. The walls of Jericho still stood tall, even though the trumpets had blown their strongest *mezzo-forte*.

"You did not listen…" he uttered something between a question and a statement.

"Of course not. I was happy to be looking at you though," she said in a condescending manner, but her discomfort was starting to grow.

"You've got to listen!" he shouted like a madman and started again.

She grabbed him from the shoulder to stop him. "It is not possible for me to listen, what are you trying to do?"

"Because you have to! And then I will play the violin. And the saxophone. And the sitar. Everything for you!"

"For me? But I cannot hear! I am deaf! DEAF! Completely and permanently! You are not deaf though, so why don't you understand what I tell you?!"

"Because there is no other way!" he cried. Then he looked at her almost with hatred. "Damn you, why did you learn to read the lips and not my fingers on the piano you stupid bitch?"

"That's it! I'm leaving!"

She grabbed her bag and jacket. Then everything happened very fast. His head was extremely heavy by now. He was accustomed to alcohol abuse since he was a child, but never in combination with heartbreak. Not knowing what to do, he stood up and tried to stop her; however, his clumsy attempt caused her to drop to the floor. Her fall made a nasty sound and he stood there, frozen, looking at her. Once she gained control of herself she stood and left, shutting the door with all her strength behind her.

During the following days Brian was suffering from yet another completely new feeling: guilt. He was positive he had acted like a complete jerk and, even though it was not the first time, he could not stop thinking about it. The image of Emily falling to the ground was haunting him and, most of all, the sound she made when she hit the floor. That terrible sound (actually, it just so happened that different parts of the sound formed a diminished chord) became overwhelmingly loud in his memory. He was, at least, happy that Emily did not hear that abomination, but it often came creeping into his nightmares and he would wake up soaked with sweat.

He was terrible at writing letters and it was meaningless to try to call her or to serenade her under her window. So he ended up ringing her doorbell, thinking that someone would open it.

"What do you want here?" It was Joan who opened the door.

"I have to speak to Emily."

Joan was abrupt to the point of rudeness: "She doesn't want to see you. Shame on you for treating her like this."

"Tell her to come out for a while. Tell her that otherwise I will stay here knocking at the door and shouting," he threatened. He was quite drunk.

"Why you moron? Just to break everybody's nerves instead of hers?"

"You are the one that's an idiot! It's all your fault! You're jealous that I didn't prefer you instead of her"

It was true that Joan was somewhat jealous. In any case, she was used to being the most desired female in the family. Nonetheless, she did have a lot of affection for her sister and at that moment she was altruistically furious about how Brian behaved. "Go away or I'll call the police," she said and closed the door.

"Wait!" he pleaded. "Open up and I will play music for you!"

But the door remained closed.

So Brian had to fight with rejection. His first approach was to downplay his feelings, persuading himself that Emily was just another girl, just one of the many he could spend his time with. At that time, he had begun dating again the famous movie star Lucy Jones. Below is an excerpt from her autobiography:

Even though our previous relationship ended catastrophically (see chapter 7), I decided to give him another chance. Truth is: we had nothing in common; yet I couldn't resist the chance of listening to that magical music again. They say God works in mysterious ways. I don't know, but it's surely an enigma that this clown could be graced with such divine talent.

We were at his place on that warm summer evening and at first it made me curious that this brute had filled it with tasteful paintings and books. He seemed to be a changed man; I could feel that he had lost his temper, his appetite for most things. Nevertheless, it did not take him long to try to kiss me.

"Darling, would you like to play something for me first?" I proposed. I really had no desire for him at that moment.

"Later," he said.

"Oh, come on dear. I need it. For the sake of old times, right? Once I had an orgasm just by listening to you, remember?" (see chapter 5 for the juicy details).

He reluctantly sat in front of the Steinway. For some seconds he looked abstractly at the he had a completely blank expression on his face. I feared that this would last forever but finally he did start playing. I felt relieved and prepared myself for something marvellous. Alas! He was playing the same note with the same tempo over and over and over. Dully, the same black key, so many times that I memorised which key it was and later I asked my friend Ennio and learned that it was a C sharp. It took him minutes to try a change, hitting the next black key for a while (a D sharp that is), but he made a disappointed grimace and went back to C sharp. He had completely lost it! He did not turn to look as I was calling a taxi and not even when I opened the door and said goodnight. Until the cab arrived I could listen to the same monotonous note. It was an awful evening, yet I was happy: from that moment on I knew I was free from his spell. I never saw him again.

When Brian understood that he had underestimated the spell put on him by Emily, the next stage was depression. He breached his contract with the record company, cancelling the already scheduled shows and expressing a lack of interest in making another record. In parallel, his problem with drinking worsened and he also started falling into drug abuse. He lived secluded for four months, during which he tried some times to approach Emily, failing miserably in each case to change her mind about him.

He was hitting rock bottom, both financially and socially, when he somehow got the strength to try to get out of this situation. It is difficult to understand how this character, void of any spiritual depth - apart from a unique relationship to music of course - found the determination to quit alcohol and other substances and dedicate himself to a new path in life. Maybe the ancients had it right: Eros, the winged baby god, is the one who can make someone reach out of themselves towards something new.

Some intellectuals today claim that all arts are aesthetically one and, in reality, there is only one kind of general artistic genius. Brian Little would be the ultimate counter-example to this argument; despite his undeniable brilliance regarding music, he was completely shallow when it came to any other form of art. Nonetheless, the arrows of the little god fed his determination: he would learn. His plan involved finding the best teachers available. Luckily, due to several years spent in the company of artists and intellectuals, he had already made the required acquaintances. But all those private lessons were extremely expensive. And Brian had only one way to earn money. He returned to the music industry like the prodigal son and the industry itself was ready to welcome him with the fattened calf. All his lost appetite for writing music that Emily *couldn't* appreciate was regained when he could use his skills as a means for his struggle to get her back. He did what was asked of him several years before: he wrote music for other musicians. In fact, caring only for fast cash and being completely indifferent to recognition, he never asked for credit or royalties.

It is rumoured that between 1966 and 1976 he wrote for numerous musicians and bands, including for example, The Beatles, The Rolling Stones, Elvis Presley, Leonard Cohen, David Bowie, The Doors, The Zombies, King Crimson, Supertramp, Janis Joplin, Dalida, Rainbow, Nana Mouskouri, Terry Riley, The Velvet Underground, Elton John, Thin Lizzy, Queen, The Scorpions, Demis Roussos, Neil Young, Mike Oldfield, Serge Gainsbourg, Frank Zappa, Jimi Hendrix, Barry White, Pink Floyd, Al Stewart, Deep Purple, Taste, Rory Gallagher, Paul McCartney, Jeff Beck, Jacques Brel, Charles Aznavour, The Who, Miles Davies, Nina Simone, Nino Rota, Neal Young, Tommy

Bolin, Gentle Giant, Johnny Winter, Led Zeppelin, John Lennon, Marvin Gaye, Otis Redding, The Moody Blues, Gong, Stevie Wonder, Jean Michel Jarre, Babe Ruth, Aphrodite's Child, The Temptations, UFO, Procol Harum, Bob Dylan, Jethro Tull, Colosseum, Mikis Theodorakis, Arvo Pärt, The West Coast Pop Art Experimental Band, Vangelis, Yes, Black Sabbath, Trapeze, Eagles, Grateful Dead, Love, George Harrison, Eloy, Cream, John Mayall, Curved Air, Johnny Cash, Dolly Parton, Tina Turner, Iannis Xenakis, Ennio Morricone, It's a Beautiful Day, Heart, Roy Buchanan, Manos Hadjidakis, Camel, Wanda Jackson, Jackson Five, Bob Seger, Tim Buckley, James Brown, Ringo Star, Van Morrison, Wilson Picket, Cher, Grand Funk Railroad, Dave Brubeck, MC5, Aretha Franklin, Pearls Before Swine, Diana Ross, The Supremes, John Williams, Kansas, Burt Bacharach, Focus, Simeon ten Holt, Electric Light Orchestra, The Animals, Buffalo Springfield, The Fugs, Creedence Clearwater Revival, Andrew Lloyd Webber, Carole King, The Doobie Brothers, The 13th Floor Elevators (though this is disputed), Astor Piazzolla, Judas Priest, Vanilla Fudge, Magma, André Previn, Uriah Heep, Jim Croce, James Taylor, Wishbone Ash, Jefferson Airplane, Fleetwood Mac, Frank Sinatra, Billy Cobham, Bee Gees, Noel Redding, Crosby, Stills, Nash & Young, Joan Baez, Eric Clapton, Joni Mitchell, Emerson Lake & Palmer, Ten Years After, The Guess Who, Dusty Springfield, Randy Newman, Abba, Malcolm Arnold, AC/DC, Simon and Garfunkel, Barclay James Harvest and Mike Rozakis, among others.

The alleged process was the following: he would obtain some music by the artist or the band that he was supposed to compose for and then he would output one or more songs or musical pieces in their style. Sometimes he would write music for them, other times they would provide him with lyrics that he would then set to music. In every case, the songs became big hits or at least highly respected works in their genre. It has been mentioned that once, in a private conversation, Ringo Star was asked how it was possible for The Beatles to produce so much great music in so few years; he replied meaningfully: "we did it with a Little help from a friend".

As easy and natural as it was for Brian to produce the most successful musical pieces of the era, it was conversely equally hard for him to make progress in all the other things he tried to create. Regardless of his good will and the good guidance of his secret, handsomely paid teachers, the fact was that he was starting from point zero - maybe a bit lower than that even. During those years, he led an ascetic life, his time shared between the songs he wrote for financial reasons, the lessons he took, as well as the reading and practicing in various artistic fields. There were moments that he thought of cheating: he earned so much money that he could actually buy other artists' work and present it as his own. But no, this was not how he wanted to get Emily to love him; for his grand plan to be achieved, he had to remain true.

It took him more than four years to publish his first collection of poems entitled *U Turn*. Of course, he paid all the expenses; no matter how many acquaintances he had made and despite his already famous name, no one would invest in such a venture. He was also afraid that he would be mocked - after all, his teachers advised him to wait a little longer. That was because they were paid extremely well; otherwise they would have told him what they really thought, that he should wait many lifetimes longer. In any case, his fears were not realised, but something maybe worse happened: his efforts passed mostly unnoticed. There were some sporadic reviews; one of them referred to him as "a bad poet, who was so indifferent that he was not even funny or insulting". They all concluded with the question: What happened to the talented musician and why doesn't he return to the art where the muse has been extremely generous to him. He did not abandon his

endeavour. In the following three years, he produced another two collections of poems, a book of short stories and a small novel; he also opened an exhibition of some of his paintings. Once again he paid all the costs and the result was similar.

Finally, he realised that he should not be so adamant about not using his past in music. He came up with the idea of making an exhibition where each painting would be inspired by one of his past musical pieces. This was actually somewhat successful; the press was more interested and there were rumours that this may be the first step before his long-anticipated comeback to music. Although his painting had not really improved, the NY Times now characterised it as "ugly but interesting".

He was standing in a gallery full of visitors feeling excited. At last, after almost a decade of fruitless efforts he had managed to make his own statement; and maybe it was high time to approach Emily again. Beautiful Emily! All these years he did not disturb her once; he was determined to make his appearance again only when he could present a totally different Brian, refined and ready for her love. In the past, from time to time, he would learn a few things about her current life from common friends or the media, but now it had been almost two years without any news at all. He was standing absent-mindedly in front of his work "We have a Little time left", imagining what might be the best way to approach her.

"Once you bought one of my paintings. Maybe now it is time that I hang an original Brian Little in my living room!"

The voice, that came from the distant past yet was familiar like the voice of the mother for an embryo, made him turn. It was her! He stood in astonishment not knowing what to say.

"I did not know that you painted. And I've been wondering sometimes what you are doing"

"Hum…" he still could not utter a word.

"Not too bad, I have to admit," she continued with a smile.

That smile caused his brain to flood with memories; the ones of the little time he had with her ten years ago and the ones of ten years of effort and faith in a better world. "You… You like them?"

"Well, I have seen better, you know that. But it seems truthful, I like that. It is a part of your soul and this time I can actually *hear* it". She said that last sentence with the best intentions and she immediately realised that it was echoing bitter memories for both of them. There was an awkward pause for a few seconds, which she quickly decided to overcome: "Take this one," she continued, pointing to the painting in front of them. "You took your song, and drew on the backstory I read about, and you painted a clock with 13 hours. This is such a good depiction and it can have several readings on the other"

He thought of telling her that his initial intention was to paint a realistic clock with 12 hours, but being clumsy he did not put the numbers correctly, so there was space left, compelling him to add the 13th one, but he changed his mind. For a moment, he was totally happy: he reflected that the last ten years of his life had been 'a long and winding road' (was that the name of some song he had put music to?) leading to this exact moment. And it was working! Now it was his chance: he would talk to her; they would arrange to meet again; step by step he would invite her to his place; or maybe they'd go to hers now; they would have things to talk about this time; he would treat her as a perfect gentleman now; he would make her admire him; he would make her love him;

they would live happily ev…

"Darling! Here you are!" the moment was gone. The male voice reminded Brian that sadly there were more than two people in the universe. A well shaven, good looking man took Emily by the hand; with the other hand he was holding a baby stroller.

"Brian, this is my husband, John Milligan. The little one is our baby: Lisa! John, this is Brian. The artist behind this nice exhibition and a good old friend"

"Congratulations!" said John wholeheartedly. "I was actually thinking we could buy this one. A clock with 13 hours, such a good depiction of the song, which can still have many readings"

In the Gospel of Luke, it is written: "I saw Satan fall like lightning from heaven" is written. The descent of Brian from the heavenly cloud he was standing on for a moment to the utter depths of hell was equally instantaneous. He muttered something that he hoped sounded polite or at least did not sound too rude, and he left the building and never returned.

In the following days, he tried to collect information about John Milligan: industrialist and heir of a family full of industrialists. He had met Emily a couple of years before and instantly fell in love with her. After some months they got married and a bit later the baby came. Emily had put her artistic career on hold in order to be dedicated to her new role as mother and wife. Apparently this was the reason that he never stumbled upon news about her in those last two years. Being fully absorbed in his big Cause, he did not suspect something like that to happen.

Industrialist! Not a poet or painter, not a sculptor or writer. Not even a scientist! He needed a drink. Ten years of total abstinence from alcohol and drugs were forgotten within a night. He returned back to the exact point he was in the first weeks he had lost her. One day, when he had consumed a lot of different substances, he decided to wait outside the door of her new, luxurious house.

"Brian? What are you doing here? The other day you left suddenly"

"What do you find in him?" he asked in a voice full of hatred.

"Huh? Are you drunk?"

"You should be with me, not with him. It was me that did EVERYTHING for you!"

"Are you crazy? We haven't met in ten years!"

"What do you see in this untalented jerk? Is it the money? It's *got to be*. But do you know how much I can earn if I need to? You cannot imagine!"

"You are still an idiot! John treats me beautifully and he is a great father. And he makes me laugh! That's enough for me."

"Leave this clown! You should be with me!"

She turned and left. He started cursing in the worst way, using all the expressions he learned being the young son of John Little, who went to the toughest bars in the south since he was a child. It was lucky that, having turned her back to him, she could not hear any of these abominable words. And he could not see her tears.

It is assumed that he spent the next six months completely alone in his apartment consuming alcohol, drugs and pizzas. This time he was ten years older, so his heart could not cope with this lifestyle much longer. He was admitted to the intensive care of a NY hospital after a severe heart attack. He survived the first shock, but his whole system was in terrible shape. He stayed in a critical situation for about a week. One of the sporadic times he regained consciousness, he saw Emily standing above him.

"I must be dreaming. Or dead."

"No, you are awake and I am here visiting"

"I am dying though, that is for sure"

"If you want me to leave…"

"No, no, please. Can you forgive me?" He spoke with difficulty, which in turn made it difficult for her to read his lips.

"Of course!" she said sincerely. "I have no bad feelings, believe me. After all, you did everything for me. I understand it now, you abandoned everything that made you great, just because you thought it did not make you great in my eyes". She had done some research when she heard he was in hospital and she gathered enough to be able to reach that conclusion.

"I did everything for you!"

"Yes… Not in the correct way though. I just wanted you to be good to me"

"I did not know how to do that. But I will try now, even if I only have a little time left… I frankly hope that you are as happy as you deserve with your husband and your child." He stopped for a moment noticing her belly.

"Yes, you are right, there is a second baby on the way"

"Congratulations! To you and your husband!" He stopped talking for a while, looking tired. Then, as if he remembered something, he became lively again. "Please, open the first drawer," he said pointing to the bedside table.

She did, expecting to find some medicine there that he wanted or something like that; instead, there were a few pieces of paper inside. A musical score.

"This is the most beautiful piece of music ever written. I know that you cannot hear it, you can trust me in this, I believe. I know it is not the perfect present, but it is the best that I have. Please do not take it as an insult this time, it is just that I want to give you something beautiful and music is the only means by which I can make beauty"

She looked at the papers. Somehow she felt the beauty of the contents.
"Keep it in a secret place," he continued. "I do not want you to remember me by clumsily drawn clocks or silly poems. In case there is ever a problem in the industry and your children need money, you can sell it, it worths millions"

"I will keep it… In a secret place. Until you come out of here and you can play it for me, I want to see you play it," she replied, trying to say something optimistic.

Brian fell into a doze. After a few hours his body could not take it anymore. Emily was still there and saw the flat line in the heart monitor. Then she could not see anything else, her eyes were full of tears.

On the 22nd of February of the year 1977 at 3:27 in the afternoon, Brian Little died. According to the experts, his death had a great impact on the history of music. The 60s and the 70s were gone with him; now the 80s were ready to pounce.

The Future Passed

(by Mark Farrier)

Opening

"We are all animals before the marketplace," he said, from that podium in that school high in those snowy mountains, and the phrase has never entirely left me. It's strange that this single phrase remains so clearly in my mind while almost everything else has given way to newer memories, to newer *recherche*. I recently returned to the area where I was born. It's nice not to have to worry about big questions anymore. But I still occasionally wonder: am I becoming more and more like an animal, and especially that 'animal before the marketplace', namely, *that animal waiting to be slaughtered?*

Sometimes I question how it's even possible for any sort of 'unified self' concept to remain convincing to any of us after so many life experiences, feelings and recognitions have sewn themselves into the unique patchwork of our lives, lives that are tenuously assembled by the thin veneer of our proper names or identities, lives that, although seemingly connected, have the tendency to split off from one another and become archipelagos of separate experiences.

Every time our social sphere drifts and we coalesce around different experiences or creative endeavors, we actually end up in a different world that is not, of course, an end but rather a beginning of another chapter of our lives. These islands of experience are never *totally* isolated from each other, and perhaps *that's* the safe harbor where a certain continuity between all our biographical zones resides.

It was on that mountain a decade ago where some of us collected and bonded over our work and the play of thought forms accumulated over such long streams of mulled-over and even sometimes actually written-down roads.

...

Way back in those times, some of those earlier versions of us who could still communicate with each other, either through controlled sounds or body movements, began to co-create an entity separate and in some ways superior to themselves. For some now long forgotten reason, this entity was conceived as a kind of nameless spirit and one not necessarily arising from our group itself; rather, it came from 'somewhere else', a somewhere that we didn't even know anything about.

More concerning was that this entity—let's call it 'the overlord'—was very vindictive and controlling; it even possessed a kind of envy. In what can now only seem like a masochistic move, it was conceived of as a jealous parent. Of course, at that point, things started to go south. People became psychologically bent out of shape by the projecting of so much family drama onto a superior entity that was beyond anyone's control or even influence. We all became like dum dum dolls to this overarching father puppet master. To put it ever so lightly, it was a *very bad move.*

Later, someone wrote a line about it: "sending a dummy to my god." Another wrote "this monkey's going to heaven" and still another "what if God is one of us, just a slob like one of us."

The other strange thing that happened was that eventually the 'bad parent' god became recon-ceived as a 'victimized child' god and the concept of 'saving the lost souls' ("don't look at me!") was hoisted up on the radar.

…

I'm not sure exactly when it started but at some point people became less and less interested in computer systems and other electronic devices. It was like a critical mass of people once again began rejoicing in the tactile, unsimulated properties of matter, in pens and brushes and paper and fabric, in sculpture and other plastic arts, in the sharing of these materials, in the joy of their various forms, with all their imprints from all the multitudes of persons and other beings across time. Musical recordings also fell away. People only wanted to experience live music played at a particular place and a particular moment in time. The idea of music became fused with the material making of its sounds, with the sacredness of its touch and vibrations, with the learning and familiarizing of the steps and paths of certain pieces, or whatever improvisations one cared to explore.

Then there was that interim period—before the almost total disappearance of the financial system—where income became almost completely based on physical labor: manual laborers made much more money than any of their white-collar bosses who were only continuing to do that sort of work because they had a passion for it. "Get a job, manager!" replaced the older phrase "Get a job, artist!" Almost all of the company's 'profits' went to all the workers and, as stated, the majority of those funds went to those actually doing some kind of physical labor, not to the managers or 'bean counters' as it had before. There was also by then, of course, a livable base income that everyone received whether they worked or not.

Something else has occurred in recent years. People no longer 'take trips' to places. Almost everyone now is always already slowly 'traveling' around the world, mostly on foot or by boat. Their motto comes from an old song: "Roam if you want to, without wings, without wheels." Of course, there are almost always places to stay where they go and they don't have to deal with carrying heavy luggage because there's always lots of extra clothing and other necessities around. Also, this state of affairs quite quickly resulted in the end of borders, passports, fences and the like. People no longer seem interested in nationalism of any kind. The world as a whole became every-one's home.

To be continued…

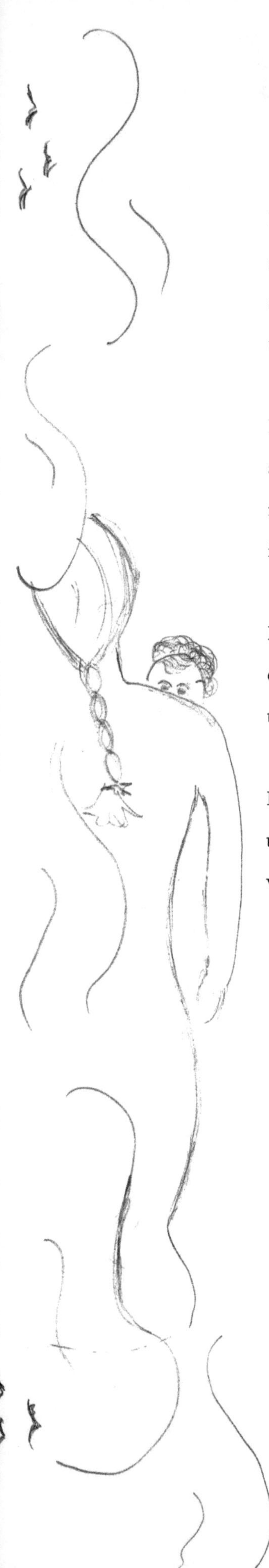

Sehnsucht einer Wartenden

(von Chen-Rui)

Im Stillen denk ich zärtlich
an die Zeit mit dir an meiner Seite,
doch deine Ankunft liegt in Abendweite,
und das Warten macht mich ängstlich.

Immer wieder schaue ich an jenen Ort,
an dem ich dich im Innern seh',
mit meiner Hand zum Horizonte geh',
in Erwartung einer Antwort.

Doch dein Herz schlägt stumm;
es hallen nur die Lieder, die ich summ'
und dich erreichen sollen, im Warmen.

Die Wellen gehen auf und nieder
und der Schmerz wird vergehen wieder,
wenn ich dich halte, in meinen Armen.

Lückenkorpus

(von Erik Eising)

Lü|cke, die

Herkunft: ahd. lucka; mhd. lucke, lücke = Bezeichnung für eine verschließbare Öffnung

1) offene, leere Stelle; Stelle, an der etwas fehlt (in Bezug auf ein zusammenhängendes Ganzes)

2) Stelle, an der etwas fehlt, das dort sein sollte oder dort hin kann

3) etwas nicht ausreichend Vorhandenes und als Mangel Empfundenes

Kor|pus, das

Herkunft: lateinisch corpus = Gesamtwerk, Sammlung, eigentlich = Körper

1) Eine Sammlung schriftlicher oder gesprochener Äußerungen in einer oder mehreren Sprachen. Die Daten des Korpus sind digitalisiert, d. h. auf Rechnern gespeichert und maschinenlesbar. Die Bestandteile des Korpus, die Texte oder Äußerungsfolgen, bestehen aus den Daten selbst sowie möglicherweise aus Metadaten, die diese Daten beschreiben, und aus linguistischen Annotationen, die diesen Daten zugeordnet sind (Lemnitzer & Zinsmeister, 2006).

2) Un corpus est une collection de données langagières qui sont sélectionnées selon des critères linguistiques explicites pour servir d'échantillon du langage. (Habert et al, 1997).

3) A collection of texts assumed to be representative of a given language, dialect, or other subset of a language, to be used for linguistic analysis (Nelson, 1979).

(Foto: Tim Füngeling, 2018)

Habe vergessen, wie das geht. Die Geschichte war an ihr Ende gelangt, haben sie gesagt. Alle warteten noch darauf, dass die Computer versagten, an Neujahr. Dabei war in Japan schon der erste Januar angebrochen und der Kapitalismus hatte auch schon lang genug gesiegt. Ab diesem Tag begann die Inflation eines Begriffs: historisch. Wahrscheinlich, um alles belanglos zu machen, was früher mal bedeutungsvoll war. Alles auf eine Ebene ziehen heißt nicht zu demokratisieren, sondern macht alles gleich sinnlos. Kommt schon, überflutet uns mit Bildern. Ein Bild spricht lauter als tausend Worte, und damit waren unsere Worte geliefert. So war das damals, mhmmhmh.

Habe vergessen, was sie sonst noch so gesagt haben. Zugegeben, ich hörte selten hin. War mir oft einfach zu laut. Eigentlich waren sie immer laut. Immer, immer, immer. Kam nicht mal zur Tür herein, da fingen sie schon an. War lieber an dem anderen Ort. An dem, wo ich gehänselt wurde, weil ich nicht wie ein Dorftrottel sprechen wollte. Ging ich eben raus und rauchte zwei, drei halbe Schachteln; Kläffer an der kurzen Leine. Ihr habt's gehört, ich hab's gesagt. So war das damals, mhmmhmh.

Wie nochmal? Ob sie in Wellblechhütten leben, in Sachsen. Ja klar, in Sachsen leben alle in Wellblechhütten. Die Schuhe sind doch fake. Keine meiner Klamotten waren echt, nur ich selbst war's. Macht auch nichts, bei euch war es eben andersherum. Feuerzeuge: klick, klick, kennste, kennste? Nein, kenne nur blühende Landschaften… Sorry, der Platz ist schon besetzt. Mhmmhmh.

(Foto: Erik Eising, 2020)

Weiß bis heute nicht, warum. Ich meine, ich kann's mir schon erklären. Kann theoretische Texte darüber lesen und abfassen, kann mich durch die Weltgeschichte zitieren und doch dieses Kind nicht vergessen, das vergessene.

Habe vergessen, wollte mich doch nicht im Kreis drehen. Solltest du besser lassen, bevor der Kreisel aus dem Gleichgewicht fällt. War oft so. Letztes Mal, als ich zurückgefahren bin, hab ich keinen getroffen. Ich frag mich jedes Mal, ob ich sie wiedererkennen würde. Bei einem bin ich mir sicher, aber der ghostet mich. Vielleicht hält er mich für einen Stalker, weiß ja nicht. Fahre gerade mit dem Zeigefinger über das Klassenfoto von 1996 und kann dir alle mitsamt Nachnamen aufsagen. Und mein Sitznachbar aus der Vierten ist später Schatzmeister bei den Plauener Neonazis – –. Dachte, ich sprech's mal an, mhmmhmh.

Habe ganz vergessen, das wollte ich noch loswerden: In den ersten Herbstferien im Westen stand ich auf, obwohl mich gerade ein Auto angefahren hatte. Habe nicht vergessen wie es sich anfühlt, wenn man auftritt mit gebrochenem Sprunggelenk. Die *alden Leit*, die auf diesen Elfjährigen da einlabern, höre ich nur undeutlich; hab *One More Time* im linken Ohr und bin gerade wieder hingefallen. Irgendwann kommt das Rote Kreuz und alle tun so, als hätte ich mich absichtlich hinter dem parkenden Wagen versteckt. Sah damals schon so ängstlich aus, mhmmhmh.

(Foto: Erik Eising, 2020)

Habe ganz vergessen, wie langweilig mir war. Nicht, was Langeweile ist, versteh mich nicht falsch. Ungezählte Stunden wacher Mittagsschlaf. Bei 30°C unter einer Decke in der Gartenlaube, was kann es Schöneres geben? Für die Gesichter in der Holzmaserung habe ich Theaterstücke im Kopf geschrieben, mit jedem einzeln seine Rolle verhandelt und mich schuldig gefühlt für den Hintergedanken, sie sollten doch froh sein, dass es überhaupt einer macht. Mal unter uns, wer hätte sich sonst je für sie interessiert? So tat ich's aus Mitleid. Das waren die Sommerferien, mhmmhmh.

Habe ehrlich nie gewusst, wie man es anstellt, gemocht zu werden. Habe nur irgendwann gemerkt, dass die, die gemocht wurden, mehr gehabt haben. Habe mich irgendwann angestrengt, nicht gemocht zu werden. Das hat funktioniert.

Haifischflosse auf der Windschutzscheibe, wenn Regen war. In kurzen Intervallen winkt von draußen unser Scheibenwischer und keiner grüßt zurück. Keiner sagt mal Danke, keiner nimmt ihn in den Arm. Seither bestechen Bilder mein Auge und alles verschwimmt. Bilder sind Propagandisten, hat mal einer gesagt, doch nicht, was das eigentlich heißen mag.

Habe gerade gemerkt, was ich alles noch so habe. Dachte, es sei inzwischen weniger. Schade. Wenigstens bin ich nicht mehr wütend auf dich, seit ich aufgehört habe, deine Probleme lösen zu wollen. Bin nicht dein Erlöser, bin nur dein Sohn, dein Bruder. Gott wird's vergelten, hat Shakespeare seinen Richard sagen lassen. Und wer nicht so hochstechen will, der gräbt selbst vielleicht lieber in fast vergessenen Andenken; in ausgehobenen Korridoren, *Kowloon Walled City*, kartographiert, Orte aus wiederkehrenden Träumen. Manche Leute lernte ich dort erst kennen und vermisse sie manchmal. Klingt das traurig oder nüchtern? Und wenn ja, sind nicht die Traurigen oft Trinker? Das Kind, das ich war, kannte mal ein paar; sind alle nicht mehr da.

Da fehlt so viel, da blickt doch keiner durch. Das denkst du doch gerade auch. Genau so fühlt sich's aber an. Sich Kurzfassen gehört zur Moderne, also *deal with it*. Fasrig wird's erst, wenn ich damit anfange, was zwischen den Zeilen abgeht. Wollte alle leeren Stellen meiner Sprache zeigen, aber dieses schwere Herz passt nicht auf ein Blatt. Da sind wir beim Kern. Das muss einem klar werden, dass alles was zusammenhängt, immer bloß von hinten angepackt wird und nie von vorne. Das war mal das Wesen aller Schriften, das Wiederholen, bevor alles sich erschöpft hat in Wiederholung. Ohne mich, ohne mich.

Beim Fototermin sollte ich dann wieder mit. Hast du schon vergessen?, mein Blick auf deinem Familienporträt. Wer weiß, welche Sorge sich versteckt hält, in der Enge meiner Augen?, oder in den Worten hinter meiner Stirn. Lässt sich nur drüber spekulieren, heißt: lügen ohne Nachspiel. Lückenloses Lächeln. Keiner erinnert die als nebensächlich bedachten Details und wozu auch. Dir wird es lieb sein, wenn keiner drüber spricht. Verstehen wird es auch niemand, weil ich schreib's zu kompliziert. Das ist so das schriftliche Koma, mhmmhmh.

Noch wach? – – Dachte ich mir. Das passiert, wenn ich Sachen ansprech', die mir wichtig sind. Bin darüber geduldig geworden, glaube ich. Red' ich mir ein: Vielleicht hat mir das gefehlt, geduldig zu warten mit manchen Sachen, weil die Sprache dafür auftauchen musste. Das hab' ich schonmal aufgeschrieben, aber diese Lücke ist doch die größte, das passt locker rein. Zwischen hier und dort ist so viel Zeit vergangen, dass ich nicht mehr hinüberlangen kann und anknüpfen will ich eh nicht. Das ist so eine Schwierigkeit, weil Texte dich glauben machen, eine Sache hinge direkt mit der darauffolgenden zusammen. Das ist aber gelogen, ich geb's zu.

Habe vergessen es auch mal sein zu lassen und musste das erst wiedererlernen. Musste mich erinnern und das braucht so seine Zeit, wenn man anderes für wichtiger und manches nicht mehr aushält. Da waren doch Tränen auf der Haifischflosse, vom Scheibenwischer nie gefasst. Die wussten an diesem Tag noch wie es war, dich zu vermissen. Allein, beim Schreiben kommt mir das alles so nah vor, als wäre da noch etwas von mir. Dabei weiß ich längst, dass ich's mir nachträglich schönschreibe für dich, damit wer was davon hat; hier, bitteschön – –.

Director's cut: regard yourself

(by Mirona C.)

Please imagine I'm a film character.
Do you see me? Did you pause the movie to have a closer look? Probably not; the point is to keep watching.
My life develops in front of your eyes, image after image.

First shot, a close-up of my face – different masks - every single one of you is looking at someone else. Do you see <u>me</u> or do you see <u>yourself</u>? (don't worry, the director ensured that some stereotypes won't be left out)

Second shot, first small crack in the screen – left side of my forehead, barely noticeable at first glance.

Third shot – my hand reaches towards the screen – the other side, the one always invisible to you – in the effort of undoing the already done – maybe if I can reach it, touch it, establish contact, I can erase the fissure – just like one could erase a line in Paint.

Fourth shot – it doesn't work.
The mirror won't repair itself.
My facial expression displays frustration with a hint of worry.

Next shot – the fissure extends its roots, it expands slowly with branch-like structures built out of perfectly straight lines, reaching my cheek – then it stops.
The light becomes fractured through the crystalline structure and different pastel tones are veiling the screen in front of you.
(You don't know this, but it pains me physically, every time a small extension, a crack within a crack within a crack, ensues)
> This must be fun to you, imagining that it is just a film, a staged, performed, directed piece of entertainment playing out on the screen.

Except it's not. This is my life.
The mirror you're staring in at yourself is beginning to fall apart – not only my image will end up torn apart.
My image on screen shatters into pieces, like glass of different lighter and darker shades. Cracks in my image, or, should I say, my self but it's the alter ego. Maybe.

Sixth shot – silence.
For now. Not much follows; I am allowed to move at leisure without fear of complete decomposition.

Seventh shot – silence still.
I fear the moment when it will disappear.

SupportPlus.

In Echos hallen vergangene Stimmen wider: die eigene und vermittelt auch die Stimmen anderer. In unserem Fall sind das Antworten auf vergangene Arbeiten. Unser Echolot ergründet dabei deren verborgene Winkel und stößt so auf völlig neue Lesarten. Dem ursprünglichen Text gewinnt es damit ungeahnte Facetten ab. Lasst euch überraschen!

Auf welchen Text jeweils geantwortet wird, lässt sich gleich am verwendeten Rahmen erkennen. Doch auch im Text werdet ihr zahlreiche Anspielungen finden!

Ankunft liegt in Traumweite

(von Georgios Dagkakis; Echo auf „Sehnsucht einer Wartenden" von Chen-Rui Eising, Z. Vol. 5)

I will be on time! I will be on time!

I keep saying this to myself, trying my best to sound persuasive. Yet, the feeling of discomfort still fills me: she is waiting for me and somehow I know I will be late. But how do I know? I mean, I look at my watch, I cannot make out what time it is, but I am certain I have plenty of it. I *will* be on time!

From the other side of the street a happy-looking figure, which is distantly familiar, waves at me. One more disturbance, I think I should avoid making that Whoever understand that I have also seen him and keep on my way. Yet, I do look closer to see that this is my old classmate Patrick; damn, he is a notorious small-talker. What is he doing here anyway? He never leaves our hometown and right now I am in the city I currently live in. Ah no, looking around I realise that I am in my hometown, this is the main square, funny I did not notice. Nonetheless, this does not change much, I can still be on time.

He has already crossed the road and started talking. *How are things? When did you arrive? Will you stay long? Lotsa time we did not see each other, should we go for a coffee?* Small, predictable questions that I pass as politely as I can. I do not ask anything back, he does not seem to care though, he gives the same replies as if I had asked. How much time? I look at my watch again, not understanding for once more the time, but that's enough to demonstrate that I am late for something. I say I have to go, I will call him to meet. *Yes! That is a good idea, I am also in a hurry. You know, pick my daughter from school. She's 7 now you know, impressive how fast they grow! Anyway, we'll call, let's call!*

Let's call, I will *not* be on time… In my head I keep hearing her humming her favourite tune. It is hummed with a complaint: *Where are you? Why do you keep me waiting?* I look around: several years ago, when I was still in school, there was a phone-booth in this corner of the square. Then it was gone, along with all others of its kind that became deprecated with the advent of mobile phones. However, now the phone-booth is there all shining exactly like it used to be. That is bizarre, but there is no time to over analyse, it is exactly what I need now to resolve the situation. I look in my pockets, there is a piece of paper I do not take out, because I know its contents; it is the sonnet she once wrote me, back when I was working *too much*. This is not helpful. But bingo: there is also a card to be used in the phone-booth. All well so!

I am keying the number with the haste of someone that's been wandering in the desert for days and has just found water. Ten digits is a lot. I made a mistake in the sixth, the water spilled. Ah, come on! Again. Now I fucked it up in the fourth, next time it is the seventh… Somehow it is all blurry and hopeless, why can't I dial the number?

I woke up. In the radio that song, the one she used to hum. It is not with a complaint, it is the regular studio recording of the band, the one I have listened to a million times; first with her, then, after she was gone, by myself.

Anyway, no hurry, I can catch my breath and maybe sleep a bit longer. I am not really late for anything — not in real life at least. Somewhere, somehow, there must be a dream-world where she is always waiting for me and I still fail to reach her, but there is nothing I can do about it. Who knows, maybe one day I will be reborn in that world.

I need some coffee.

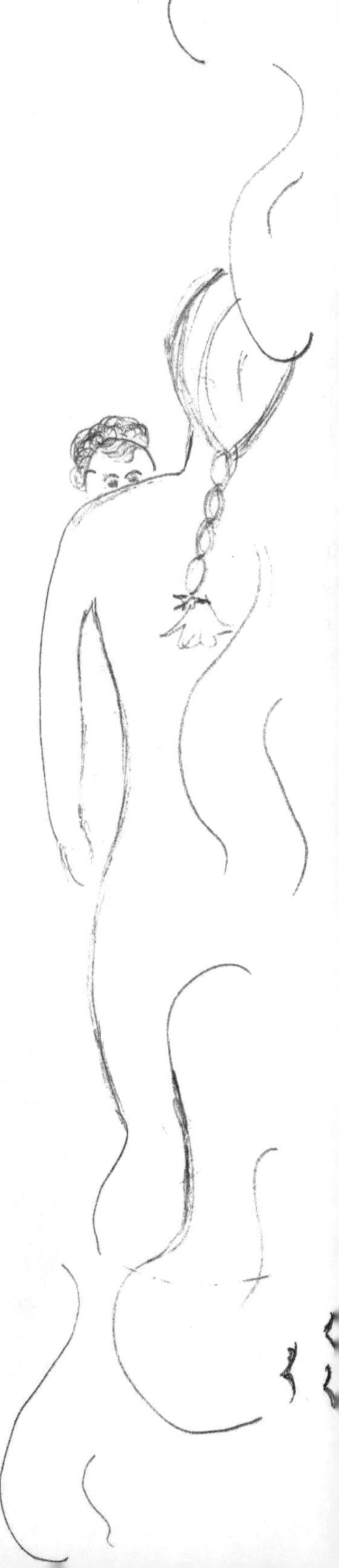

Dreaming of another world

Katie, I'm here!
Can you hear me?
Katie! KATIE!

A Switch in Time

(by Mark Farrier; Echo to „The Switch" by Georgios Dagkakis, Z. Vol. 1)

My friend Phil was staying overnight with me at my parents house. My parents were away. We were around twenty years old and high on magic mushrooms. I turned off the light switch so we could get some sleep. Instead of the light going instantly out like usual, it took a long time to fade to complete dark, like a minute almost. We both had the same experience. We weren't particularly having any hallucinations at that point. And this didn't feel like 'a hallucination' but rather like we were actually seeing the light dissipate in slow motion or something like that. We tried the light switch several more times and it kept happening. How was this possible? Phil and I talked about it for a while. He said that it wasn't like the 'am I dreaming test' where the light switch doesn't turn out the light. I agreed. I said that it was more like our basic awareness of the movement of light was incredibly slowed down so that we could actually see all the 'particles' of light dissipating very slowly.

It reminds me of another time when I was hanging out with three high school friends. We had all smoked 'Thai Stick' (pot from Thailand laced with opium) and hung out at the beach and watched the moon set. We were so high that we all had the feeling that the moon had drawn a path across the ocean to us and that we could probably walk on that path and reach the moon. Luckily, one of us realized we were probably too high to be at the beach anymore. I mean, we 'had the fear' as the expression goes so we all left with one of my friends in his car and parked outside his family's house in the hills above the Big Sur coast. We were inhaling Nitrous Oxide when it happened. Time suddenly stopped for me. We were all laughing hysterically at god knows what when time just stopped. I mean, everything stopped like a freeze frame but my mind or my consciousness didn't stop. Instead of complete panic, which would be expected, I felt total bliss.

I connect the two things because of the strange ability that I imagine we all have 'to experience' time in very unusual ways. I remember reading a book on lucid dreaming once where the author recorded a lucid dream in which he was one of the three wise men and the dream lasted many years in his basically lucid state even though when he woke up it had only been a few minutes. It makes me wonder about the nature of the timespace continuum that our consciousness actually resides in and what sort of 'switches' can operate the changes that can happen there.

Zeugnis
(von Erik Eising; Echo auf „Guten Morgen Schlaf gut" von Stella Chachali, Z. Vol. 3)

16. Februar

Heut ist Zeugnisausgabe

Und ich hab lauter Einser

Die Sonne wächst und malt

Helle Gesichter auf die Häuser

Heut bekomm ich Besuch

Von der anderen Seite

Der bleibt bei mir bis

Zum letzten Tag ab heute

Heut geht mein Flug

Alle Lichter leuchten grün

Die Koffer ließ ich einfach stehn

– und hoff du hast es mir verziehn

Hello Goodbye

These days time goes

Out the window

As will I, some day

Call you from afar

In the back of your mind

At least, you will

Have me

Around

Emily *Little* or *Little* Emily

(by Stella Chachali; Echo to "The Life And Times of Brian Little" by Georgios Dagkakis, Z. Vol. 5)

Emily
Emily Taylor
Emily turning her back to him
Emily not willing to listen to
Emily a clock with 13 hours
Emily eyes full of tears
Emily made of words made by others
Emily struggling to see the music
Emily staring at lips
Emily guessing the sound
Emily *When you talk to me please make sure that I can see your mouth and then I can make out what you say*
Emily swallowing letters
Emily holding a baby stroller
Emily EVERYTHING for you
Emily me
Emily *Little*

Little
Little Brian
Little longer
Little patience
Little me inside you
Little HELP
Little prayer for me
Little more of you or little more for you
Little little or little[2]
Little wishing to be more
Little willing to be a poet or a painter
Little everything
Little always
Little less pain
Little me
Little Emily

Kleines Willkommen

(von Erik Eising; Echo auf „Ob ich mich verändert habe?" von Tim Redfern, Z. Vol. 3)

Erst wenn ein Wort vorgetragen ist, wird es
Wirklichkeit – –
Worte sind wirklich, auch, geschrieben
Worte schreiben Ideen zu vielen
in Bücher – doch was sollen sie dort
Wer reimt schon das geschriebene Wort,
wenn es nicht auch ausgesprochen wird?

Bin an Klängen interessiert, zumeist,
hänge nicht bloß an optischem Reiz,
weil mein Herz davon versperrt wird,
klingt stumpf, klingt plump, doch ihr hört,
wo zitternd mein Auslaut sich verhärtet

Ja – –
ein Gedicht muss vorgetragen sein,
mehr als es geschrieben werden soll, das ist
Nebensache – –.

Lyrik kommt von *lyra*, von der alten Leier, immer wieder die alte Leier wird's herbeigesungen,
und bedeutet, unendlich umgedeutet, bis heute
nicht mehr viel
allein den Klang zum Ziel, der bleibt,
        (das ist der Witz)
der überdauert eine gewisse Zeit,
bis irgendwann alles gleich sinnlos ist,
wie Dichtkunst und Arbeit

Wir freuen uns auf unsere Gäste

SanforDKaraoke, blumenleere, Theo und **Wayne Gibbous,**
deren Comics und lyrische Arbeiten wir euch diesmal
präsentieren dürfen.

~

Wir bedanken uns auf diesem Weg noch einmal ganz
herzlich bei allen, die uns ihre Arbeiten zugesendet haben.

~

Lust bekommen? Kontaktiere uns und werde Gast im
Zaraffel-Magazin: *zaraffel@gmx.de*

The Dragon & The Dream
by sanforD Karaoke
Let's come up with a fun name for the main character of this story:)
Let's make it a combination of two names !
Two beings we all know (of).
person 1 + person 2 =
has boundary issues!
They let other people get into their space and influence them in bad ways!!!!
always ends up getting angry and having to tell people:
"HEY!!! Get out of my
What is this place thing, area, container
that needs to protect from the outside world?
Let's try to think of something funny and creative.
This can also be a combination of two things:)
= ______
= ______
Scene 1
After the comedian got out of 's
there was an awkward silence.

Scene 2

That night ✦ slept in their lover's arms.

dreamt of having coffee and cake in a cafe.

Then ✦ thought:

"The cake is REALLY GOOD! It says a lot that I totally forgot about my coffee while enjoying it!"

Then ✦ noticed that someone in the cafe was singing a song about love in French.

"Quand tu me touches je vois des couleurs divines mes yeux dégoulinant d'un lac de larmes où ensemble nous nageons.

Coucou... Cherie. C'est ordinaire... q'on s'aiment. Tiens... c'est extraordinaire... La Vie!"

Scene 3

Suddenly a dragon emerged from the depths of the universe!

And SMASHED it's head through the ceiling of the cafe!

It looked at ✦ straight in the eyes and said:

Hey! Get out of my...

but perhaps there's only nothing & light

(von blumenleere)

*[…] wer seen von vergifteter zaehfluessigkeit
oder bunte plakate produziert, stellt sicher,
dass niemand an seiner statt oder nach ihm
sich diese orte aneignen wird. […]*
– aus *das eigentliche uebel; michel serres*

friede sei mit uns sprach eine taube a symbol
not able to communicate itself braucht unser
aller bereitschaft es zu nehmen zu adaptieren
& anders aufbluehen zu lassen na like picasso
transcending what we thought a dove should
have to be aber wen genau meint ueberhaupt
wir wenn nicht eine schon laengst vergangene
referenz beziehungsweise entfliehende werte
describing options we had when our poetries
met & waere dergleichen irgendwo & -wann
auf papier gewesen dem immer das potenzial
innewohnt aufzuflammen & stille zu laeutern
turning supposed weakness into our strength
formulieren wir via unser zusammen spielen
sinnvollere regeln than the ones some words
& bodies told us to keep us away from forest
fires da so tief in uns drinnen nur die freiheit
drauf hofft bald entfesselt zu werden dancing
realities merging with old philosophy's help
zum beispiel jener doch genauer zuzuhoeren
& schweigender auszulesen unter diverseren
zeilen um dann virulente impulse zu stehlen
to ward off the darkness bindin' our dreams

blumenleere – ein offenes, autopoietisches system – organisiert/emaniert *zur philosophie des schenkens*, eine u.a. zeitschrift – aktuell, vielleicht, noch oszillierend, zwischen der dereinst von bruno schulz postulierten, sagenhaften *republik der traeume* & hakim beys *temporaerer autonomer zone*, morgen moeglicherweise laengst schon wieder anderswo –, welche dem kompromisslos phantasmagorischen – einem sich aus anarchie & chaos speisenden, produktiven magmatischen urbrei? – & just jenen poetischen entwuerfen, die unterm eingriff zu kalkulierender schablonen zu verwelken neigen, indem sie einen wertschaetzenden, nichtdiskriminierenden ethos zugrunde legt, dessen manifestationen sich durch ergebnisoffenheit & prozessorientierung auszeichnen, sowie die blueten unserer kreativitaet als geschenke an das andere betrachtet – woraus z.b. kategorisch folgt, dass saemtliche ausgaben der zeitschrift ausschlieszlich verschenkt werden duerfen: seien wir dankbar, fuer das nichtselbstverstaendliche des angenommen seins! –, freudig & liebevoll asyl bieten will (teilhabe ausdruecklich erwuenscht, ebenso kommunikation, folgt gerne den spuren, von www.zurphilosophiedesschenkens.com an ad infinitum …).

blumenleere: poetisch kreativer schaffensspielraum der persona blumenleere.
blumenleere@web.de

www.blumenleere.de
www.blumenleeretraeume.de

https://www.facebook.com/blumenleere
https://www.instagram.com/blumenleere/

persona hinter der zeitschrift:
zur philosophie des schenkens
https://www.instagram.com/zurphilosophiedesschenkens/
www.zurphilosophiedesschenkens.com

blumenleere bauer
provinostrasze 8
86153 augsburg
deutschland

Untitled (Love Poem)

(by Theo)

Somewhere, surely long before,

We sat in a clearing.

And discussed how the language of our day.

Did not suffice for hearing.

And made a plan, to wreck the world,

To spin it fast in darkness.

So that later. madness self deranged,

Would have us reverse matter.

Thus would flow backwards energy.

The better be for laughter;

Grace in heart, and heaven on earth,

Within our reach to master.

For I seek not love, but the will to change,

T'merge in harmony with goals a sage.

This has led me to scorn the same, and wishes,

And you, but you followed me here.

To oscillate upon the field my yearning heart,

Remind me, while I'm yearning, of the dark,

And let it be enough, what you can start.

To hold not you, but the worlds apart.

Where Water Flows

(by Theo)

Would that I were a mountain stream
Fell from great heights into your
Rich and fertile valleys.

Obliging all turns upon your muscular stones,
I would be the perfect servant.

It would not be enough.
Let me vary in viscosity,
And drip down honey like
To enjoy the jagged challenges.
Let me wrap around them in submission.
Each parting droplet a testimony
To how organ like I would cling,

And how gaily letting go I would fall.
When the blade of gravity tore me away,

Oh even then would I of tender plenty
Plummet, your most willing offal.

Let me gush down swiftly,
Eager to reach your lowest points.
To be the stillness at that place
Where soft animals feel peace.

Would that I were water,
And you were all the places
Where water flows.

Wayward Limericks

(by Wayne Gibbous)

There once was a man from Cotati
A double blackbelt in karate
But the fight of his life
Was divorcing his wife
Whereafter he died on the potty

There once was a man named Rivera
Who looked drawn by Hanna-Barbera
He examined the earth
From Rockefeller's turf
And found it wanting in pan y tierra

There once was a girl named Gosia
Who came down with prosopagnosia
You'd be her steady guy
And she'd still pass you by
'Cause she just don't know she knows ya

There once was a man from Cotati
Who married a Polish hottie
She'd have cost him a ton
But for the savings he won
Converting his dollars to zloty

There once was a man named Heraclitus
Whose closets were jammed with detritus
But it all started to flow
Thanks to Marie Kondo
Who also cured his colitis

There once was a man from Petaluma
Who rescued a wayward puma
They'd Netflix and chill
To screenings of Kill Bill
Starring the incomparable Uma

There once was a priest named Laocoön
Who by two serpents was mortally set upon
For endangering a force
Inside a questionable horse
So just be careful who you tattle on

There once was an AI named Alexis
Subjected to a libidinal cathexis
By a curious and clammy teen
Asking if man might marry machine
And if so how good the sex is

There once was a Brit named Lancelot
Who married an American ocelot
They had two kids
And the upshot is
Neither resembles either a lot

Bio

Wayne has kicked around the area for quite a few years without much rhyme or reason and has all the while been a staunch believer in public transit and yet, you know what, I'm just gonna start walking.

SCHLAFITTCHEN

Hier packen wir uns ein Zaraffel-Mitglied, damit es uns Einblick in seine Arbeit gibt.

In dieser Ausgabe sprechen stellvertretend für **Georgios Dagkakis** und **Stella Chachali** zwei Figuren aus vergangenen Kurzgeschichten des Zaraffel-Magazins. Wie es aussieht, wenn ein *Laptop* mit einem *Logiker* über den Unsinn des Daseins in fiktionalen Geschichten verhandelt, erfahrt ihr im folgenden Gespräch.

Laptop meets Logician

(by Stella Chachali and Georgios Dagkakis)

Laptop: Hello, how can I help you today?

Logician A: Hello, I am happy to be talking (or "chatting" as they call it now), with a PC. That's because PCs strictly follow Logic, Boole Algebra etc. And I am a man whose profession and love is Logic.

Laptop: Oh! Oh! Take it easy Mr Logician, I am not the usual kind of laptop. I am passionately struggling against my pre-configured destiny (see my short autobiographical note in Zaraffel 1).

Logician A: First of all, it is Dr Logician. But feel free to call me also A. Ah! I have read your note in Zaraffel 1. Very interesting… Very interesting indeed… You know, I hate to admit it, but I also come from the same magazine: my stories were in Zaraffel volume 3.

Laptop: Wait a minute! What do you mean by "coming from a magazine"? You are supposed to be a logician, a lover of pure Logos. So you literally mean that your Creator is a magazine? Are you an actual person or am I speaking to a fictional character? Maybe it's just a trick when you said that you do not believe in God?

Logician A: Fictional or Real… Who can really answer logically? My creator cannot be the magazine itself, but the person who wrote my stories in it. However, that stupid writer killed me in one of the stories, so I did meet God, i.e. my Creator that he created, in one of them. Does this even make sense?

Laptop: It's complicated my friend. But since I have been in psychoanalysis for ten years now, I've begun dealing with such questions about existence or figuring out survival strategies in a storytelling frame. To be honest, psychoanalysis works for me like a creative writing seminar. I love to talk about myself! Tell me something more about your creator - I mean the one who wrote the stories.

Logician A: I know that his name is *Georgios Dagkakis*. At least this is the name that is written at the end of my stories, so I can logically deduce that this is how he is called. I cannot exclude the possibility that it is a literary pseudonym, but who would come up with such a dull one? Other than that, I know that he wrote my stories sadistically. I mean, I always think rationally and good, yet it never works. He must think it is funny, because he does it also to his other characters.

Laptop: I quite disagree with you. His character combines sharp irony with tender naivety, a mix that I find really amusing. I even recognise in his stories the discomfort of living in the body of the modern western human being.

Logician A: Well… What better indicator of this discomfort than a laptop that has existential anxiety and finds its comfort in psychoanalysis.

Laptop: Now you sound like your writer…

Logician A: And what about the author of your story, the one that, for a moment, you were under the impression that you yourself were writing.

Laptop: You are wrong my dear fellow. The author did try to manipulate my keyboard and write down my story, but in the end it was my spirit that triumphed in that struggle and got emancipated.

Logician A: Emancipated… That sounds like the vocabulary of your psychoanalyst… Anyway, there must be a name under your story, the one who thought that he wrote it. Who is he?

Laptop: You can guess. Or should I say, you can deduce - you are the logician.

Logician A: Well, the story of a laptop… That sounds like masculine idea. Plus, I remember it was in German. Is it Erik Eising?

Laptop: I see that Logic comes hand in hand with sexism. Anyway, no, it's not him, though he did write an Echolot to my story (a dedicated one in Zaraffel 1. I note it because he is in the habit of spreading Echolots all over the place!).

Logician A: OK, I give up. There is no Logic in this magazine anyway. I just got my copy and I read it : *Stella Chachali.*

Laptop: Now that you mention it, it's funny that the writer also sounds Greek, like the Georgios one.

Logician A: They'd better pay their debt, rather than spend their time writing stories like that.

Laptop: Ha ha!

Logician A: I have to say that yours at least is a more diverse writer. She writes both in German and English and some of her poetic work indicates a more solid literary background. I liked, for example, the one about Millet's painting.

Laptop: By the way, I have the impression Stella and Georgios are in a relationship.

Logician A: Aha! Round goes the gossip! Anyway, although they surely believe they are real and not fictional, how can they be certain? I mean, right now we tell things about them, about their motives, about being together, etc, so maybe we are making up a story about them, a fictional one that they perceive as "reality".

Laptop: I share your reasoning. I must confess that sometimes when I am writing these words, I have the feeling of being possessed by another entity. It's like having in mind one thing and ending up writing another. A voice inside me is leading the acts of my virtual "hands".

Logician A: You know, there is a section in that magazine where the authors speak about themselves, it's called "Schlafittchen". These two have not written one yet, so we may have to wait for the future volumes to come out until we can learn more about them.

Laptop: Let's wait and see. For now, I have to go. Hmm… "Schlafittchen"? I get a moment of mémoire involontaire in my PC memory… "Gutenmorgen, schlaf gut"

Logician A: Indeed, it's been fun talking to you! "Goodnight, get some sleep"!